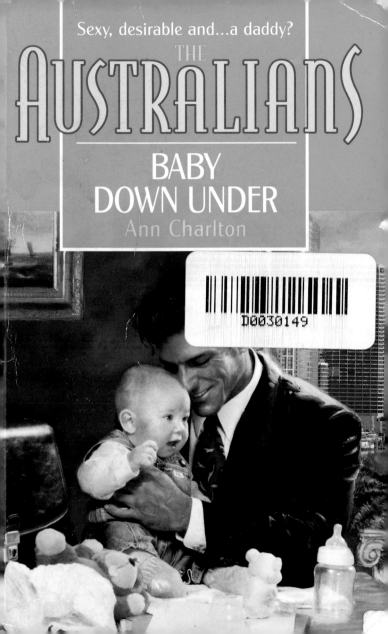

Sexy, desirable and...a daddy?

THE AUSTRALIANS

BABY DOWN UNDER

Ann Charlton

D0030149

ISBN 0-373-82580-3

9 780373 825806

50450

Welcome to Harlequin's great new series,
created by some of our bestselling authors
from Down Under:

THE AUSTRALIANS

Twelve tales of heated romance and adventure—
guaranteed to turn your whole world upside down!

Travel to an Outback cattle station, experience the
glamour of the Gold Coast or visit the bright lights
of Sydney where you'll meet twelve engaging young
women, all feisty and all about to face their biggest
challenge yet...falling in love.

And it will take some very special women to tame
our heroes! Strong, rugged, often infuriating and
always irresistible, they're one hundred percent prime
Australian male: hard to get close to...but even
harder to forget!

The Wonder from Down Under:
where spirited women win the hearts of
Australia's most independent men.

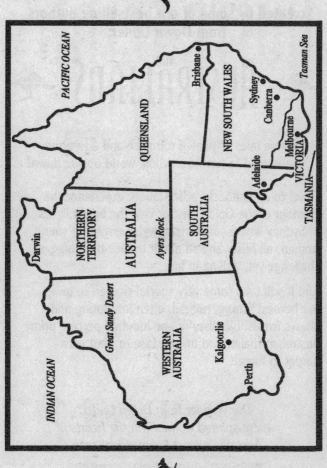

THE AUSTRALIANS

BABY
DOWN UNDER
Ann Charlton

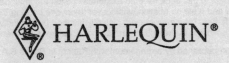

HARLEQUIN®

TORONTO • NEW YORK • LONDON
AMSTERDAM • PARIS • SYDNEY • HAMBURG
STOCKHOLM • ATHENS • TOKYO • MILAN • MADRID
PRAGUE • WARSAW • BUDAPEST • AUCKLAND

ISBN 0-373-82580-3

BABY DOWN UNDER

First North American Publication 1999.

Printed in U.S.A.

Ann Charlton wanted to be a commercial artist but became a secretary. She wanted to play the piano but plays guitar instead, and she never planned to be a writer. From time to time she abseils, which surprises her because she is afraid of heights. Born in Sydney, Ann now lives in Brisbane. She would like to do more tapestry work and paint miniatures and has absolutely no plans to research a book in the Amazon or to learn to play the bouzouki.

CHAPTER ONE

HER windscreen-wipers, sweeping at a frenzied speed, gave Alexandra a series of split-second views through the teeming rain. *Sweep.* A yellow umbrella bobbing past on the footpath. *Sweep.* Under it, the pale face of its owner, caught in the deluge. *Sweep.* Her white letterbox marking her own driveway. *Sweep.* A parcel at the door under her front steps.

Maybe this was the shipment of books she'd been waiting on for three weeks. It wouldn't be the first time the auctioneer had freighted them to her home instead of the shop.

The air smelled of hot electricity, wet grass, eucalyptus and Sam's goats. She set the van at a crawl along the drive and as she passed close by the house, saw that the parcel was too irregular to be a carton of books.

Alexandra scowled. Maybe it was another of Sam's practical jokes. Her neighbour was old enough to know better but he just couldn't resist schoolboy pranks.

She parked around the back, and dashed under cover to unlock the door to the internal stairs, a plastic shopping bag draped over her head in a futile attempt to keep her hair dry. Upstairs in the bathroom, she sighed at her reflection.

One hint of subtropical humidity and it frizzed upward and outward, like some wild, rust-coloured fleece. In Brisbane, in January, that meant every day.

After a cool shower, she dragged a brush through her hair to discourage the curl, pulled on a singlet top, a calf-length cotton skirt and, barefoot, went downstairs to look at the parcel.

More a bundle really, tucked all around with some patterned cloth. She stared at the shadows beneath the plum trees along the dividing fence.

'Sam? Come and deactivate this little booby trap of yours. You're going to get very wet if you're lurking there to see me touch it.' No answer. She turned on the light and cupped her hand to shout through the rain. 'Did you hear me, Sam? If this turns out to be one of your talking pumpkins—'

The bundle twitched. She jumped backwards, knocked over a clay pot of herbs. 'It's alive!' Eyes fixed on the cloth-wrapped shape, she fumbled around in the herbage to right the pot.

'Sam!' she yelled. 'If this is a cane toad you've left gift-wrapped under my stairs, I swear I'll—'

The bundle wailed. Chills ran down Alexandra's spine. The wail turned into a cry. She knelt and cautiously removed the towel, tugged at the tight wrappings. A fist shot out and quivered.

'Oh, God—' Alexandra stared at a tiny, reddening face. 'A baby.' She dithered, then as its cries escalated, picked it up and laid it to her damp shoulder. The child's fluff of dark hair tickled her neck. 'Ssssh, ssssh, there now,' she murmured, stroking the infant. The child quietened.

'You call me?' Sam's voice came out of the plum tree shadows. His torch made a misty nimbus through rain and she saw a bony leg hitch over the fence. 'About time. You've decided the age difference doesn't matter. You've come to your senses and realised that a woman of your taste and discrimination deserves a man who's been around a bit.'

Sam was seventy-five. He came over to the front steps, in short oilskins, walking as always as if he'd just got off a horse. Peering through the stairs, he stopped.

'That's a baby!'

'It was here, on the doorstep. Under the stairs. I thought it was a box of books.'

'Nope. That's definitely a baby.' He gave a wheezy laugh, ducked under the stairs to peer at the infant.

'But where did it come from, Sam?'

'Where babies usually come from,' Sam said dryly. 'And it wasn't Mr. Stork that dumped it at your door.'

Alexandra looked along the street, desperate to conjure up a mother. But there was nobody, only the pedestrian who had still made little progress. The umbrella disappeared behind trees and re-emerged before Alexandra's brain made the connection.

'The yellow umbrella!'

She transferred the baby to a startled Sam and loped down the steps, down the drive, down the street, into the downpour, propelled by outrage and panic. How *dare* that woman leave a baby on *her* doorstep? But the storm had brought down a shower of twigs and seeds to torture her bare feet, rain spattered her glasses, blinding her, and she soon had to give up. A few cars and a bus passed by at the end of the road but no pedestrians with or without yellow umbrellas. She hobbled back home in the rain, motherless.

Sam transferred the baby to her with alacrity. 'You'd better get the wrappings off, change its nappy or something.'

'Shouldn't we call the police?'

'Don't think they change nappies.' Sam snickered and as the child's screams amplified, said, 'Maybe it's hungry. You put some milk on to heat and I'll go get one of my kid's bottles.'

'Goats, he's talking about,' Alexandra said to the baby as he hunched into his slicker and ventured into the rain. 'He keeps goats. That's why there's always such a smell in the air around here.' The baby screamed louder. 'All

right, all *right,* we'll sterilise the bottle before we give
it to you, honest!'

She went inside, through the room down under that
she used as an office and for storing and sorting books,
and upstairs to the living room where she looked around
for a safe place to put the child. In the end, she laid it
on a rug on the floor.

'What am I going to do with you?'

The baby kicked its rug off and, finding its fist near
its mouth, sucked away. In the lull, Alexandra polished
raindrops from her glasses, towelled herself dry and
pulled socks and her Doc Martens onto her sore feet.
She hunted out a small towel that might be used as a
diaper. With this over her shoulder, she looked up the
police emergency number, picked up the phone.

'I want to report an abandoned—' No. She glanced at
the infant. 'Abandoned' was a word no baby should
hear. 'I want to report a lost child,' she rehearsed under
her breath, index finger poised to punch out the number.
'Or a lost parent.'

But the baby bellowed and looked so pathetically
small and alone on the floor so Alexandra put the phone
down again and went to it. Kneeling, she tore off the
tapes of the disposable napkin and released an aroma
that made Sam's goats smell positively sweet. Tucked
into the waist was a scrap of paper on which was
scrawled a message.

*Dear Miss Page, You saved those other kids, please
help.* Her stomach churned. She didn't want to read on,
felt the fleeting, shameful wish to remain uninvolved,
but this time she was no anonymous passer-by. This time
she, Alexandra Page, was being appealed to directly. *I
am desperate and out of my mind. Please don't let the
police or welfare know and keep my baby safe for me
until I come back in a few—* The note ended abruptly
on a damp, torn margin. A few what? Hours, days?

Weeks? She turned the note over to a blank. *I am desperate and out of my mind.* Alexandra picked up the rug and shook it. Another fragment of paper fell out. *—find him at the Blue Parrot. He is—* Here a piece was torn away and the message resumed on the next line *—and his name is Riley—* That was all. She butted the two pieces together and saw there was a triangular piece missing. 'Riley,' she said. She was not the only person named in the note. Absurdly, it relieved her, made the sense of responsibility less burdensome knowing there was someone else to share it.

But no other fragments turned up in the rug, or in the baby's clothes. She braced herself and gingerly searched the soiled napkin for further traces, but if the missing bit had been there it had succumbed to some powerful chemical forces.

She removed the offending napkin and dropped it in a bucket. By the time she had grappled with pins to secure the towel on the baby's bottom, Sam's footsteps could be heard on the front stairs. The flyscreen door opened and slapped shut and Sam came in with two bottles and a variety of teats all still in their original wrappers.

'It's a girl,' Alexandra announced.

'Gee, I should have brought some cigars,' said Sam with a snort of laughter.

He bent his bony knees and read the torn note, gave a whistle. 'You've called the police?'

Alexandra felt a wave of foreboding again. 'I'll do it as soon as we've given the child some milk.'

It was the sensible thing to do. The authorities were the proper people to care for an abandoned child. They could locate the mother or father.

'Why me?' she said plaintively.

In the kitchen, Sam was busy filling a bottle. '"Dear Miss Page, you saved those other kids—"' She must have seen that bit in yesterday's newspaper about you and the medal. Or on telly.' Alexandra's repressive glare failed to silence Sam on this sensitive subject. He thought it was modesty that made her so reticent.

'At least she tried to dump the kid with someone with a bit of backbone, that's in her favour,' said Sam. '"Bookseller Braves Blaze,"' he quoted. '"Intrepid Alexandra Page of Rochedale Wins Brave Conduct Medal." She probably looked up the rest of your address in the phone book. And if that was her out in the street, lurking with the brolly, she would have seen the bookstore name on the van. Must have hung about to make sure you found the poor little ferret before the neighbourhood dogs did.'

Alexandra bit back a hysterical laugh at the idea of being looked upon as a model of fortitude, the kind of woman who would never shrink from responsibility and duty.

'No one in their right mind would expect a stranger to accept a responsibility like this,' Alexandra said, staring at the screwed-up face of the baby girl. Her fine, dark hair stood straight up as if it was electrified. Alexandra felt a definite bond.

'Daft.' Sam brought over the milk. He sprinkled a bit on the back of his hand to test the temperature, then handed Alexandra the bottle.

'Notifying the authorities is for her own good,' Alexandra said. 'The mother's, I mean. The sooner she is found, the better. She must need help.'

At the approach of the bottle, the baby stopped crying and eagerly turned to it. A magnificent silence ensued. Halfway through the bottle, her hunger abating, the baby looked up at Alexandra with large, solemn blue eyes. Curious, trusting.

Dear Miss Page, I'm desperate and out of my mind.

Clearly, it was in everyone's best interests to turn this

child over to the police. The baby continued to inspect Alexandra and her tiny mouth stretched at the corners before she suddenly closed her eyes and resumed feeding. It wasn't even a smile probably, just some quirk of an immature nervous system, Alexandra told herself. The baby made tiny contented sucking noises and weighed next to nothing in her arms.

'Sam.'

'Yeah?'

'What do you think "Blue Parrot" might be?'

The Blue Parrot looked like every movie set of a jazz cellar. Bare brick walls, miniature tables, patrons shoulder to shoulder at the bar. Everything in soft focus. Minimum light, maximum smoke. Alexandra felt the allergic reaction start in her throat. Her nasal membranes began to sting. Oh, great.

'Excuse me,' she said, pushing in to speak to the bar attendant. 'I rang earlier about someone called Riley.'

'He's playing. Over there.'

'Over there' was a raised space occupied by a jazz quartet. She counted three bald heads.

'Riley's on piano,' the barman said. The crowd applauded as the saxophonist finished a solo. Alexandra heard the pianist before she saw him. He was a dim shape hunched down over the keyboard. A cigarette glowed in the corner of his mouth. Terrific, a smoker, just what she needed. Alexandra took out a tissue, raised her glasses and dabbed her watering eyes.

'Mr. Riley, I need to talk to you about a baby,' she rehearsed under her breath as she slid through the enthusiasts to take up a position by the piano. Perhaps that was too confronting. *Riley—he is—* What? The baby's father? But if the mother was in such straits as to abandon the child, he might not be keen to acknowledge his paternity. 'About a delicate matter,' she amended.

She leaned forward, raised her voice. 'Mr. Riley.'

'Sssh.' The fans scowled, shocked that she would interrupt a musician during his solo. Alexandra flushed but held her ground. Her nasal passages were worsening by the minute and she had to get out of here quickly.

'Mr. Riley!' she hissed, and again came the sharp admonitions from Riley's admirers. Riley himself showed no sign of hearing anything but his music. He bent low over the keyboard. From where she watched, there was nothing to see but hunched shoulders, the top of his head and his hands moving on the keys in a series of rapid, loverlike caresses. He had, she thought distractedly, as she groped in her shoulder-bag for a fresh tissue, more hair than the rest of the band put together. It was darkest brown, very thick, wavy and overlong at the back of the neck.

His solo finished and the other instruments came in strongly but he stayed in his trance, not acknowledging the applause. Ash fell from his cigarette as he fingered the closing segment of the number. Somewhere in the moody improvisations Alexandra caught the fugitive notes of the melody. What was the name of the song? Her impatience grew.

At last the music stopped. The band took a recess. The applause died away.

'Mr. Riley,' Alexandra said again as he sat up and flexed his shoulders forward, a performance at least as riveting as his piano playing. That white shirt would split its seams if he expanded his back any further. He reversed the process, linked his hands behind his head and put the strain briefly on his shirt buttons instead. She had some keyhole glimpses of dark chest hair.

'You the one making all the fuss?' he said, cigarette clamped in the corner of his mouth.

Dark, horizontal brows, a crease between them to attest to years of frowning. Eyes, almost invisible, squinted against the smoke. Nose, prominent and broad-bridged, rivalling a big jaw for dominance. Thin upper lip, slightly fuller lower. Okay for a man, but heaven help the baby if she took after him. If the baby was his, of course. Alexandra stared at him as she tried to remember her rehearsed opening.

'Are you old enough to be in a place like this?' he asked without much interest. 'You'll have to produce ID if you want to order a drink.'

'I don't want a drink—I want to talk to you.'

'What about?'

'It's—um—can we go somewhere private?'

He eyed her with that distinctive kind of male speculation, as if she'd invited him to her *boudoir*. Alexandra found her irritation increasing in ratio with the discomfort in her nose and eyes.

'Give me a clue, sweetheart,' he said carelessly, dropping his right hand to the keyboard where it rippled off several notes as if of its own accord. A square, powerful hand with very well-kept fingernails and no nicotine stains that she could see.

When she looked up, that narrowed but intense gaze was on her, not because he was really seeing her, just checking her reaction to *him*. He might have been a magician who'd manipulated his audience's attention and now only awaited the applause. Used to being admired, she guessed, used to people being impressed by his expertise.

But Alexandra had been around brilliance and expertise all her life. Without meaning to, she gave a faint shrug as if to say, "Nothing special." His attention sharpened and she took advantage of it to say clearly, 'I've come about a baby.'

His head tilted back. He removed the cigarette from his mouth and took a long look at her rimless glasses, her hair quelled by several circuits of a scarf twisted about her head. At her long skirt and the oversized white shirt she'd pulled on over the singlet top. She had not bothered with make-up before rushing here and she just knew that her nose and eyes were pinker than her mouth.

'A baby.' The eyebrow went up again. 'You've got one? Or you want one?'

She blinked. 'What?'

'Let me guess—you want your child to be musical and now you've heard me play—' He paused and repeated that casual little ripple of notes that seemed to play directly down the back of her neck. '—You think my genes and yours just might produce a child prodigy.' The bass player snickered at this bit of sexist wit. 'I have to tell you what I told the other one last month—sorry, no can do.'

The *other one?* Oh, dear, the poor man was pestered with women dying to have his baby.

'I've already got a baby,' she said, abandoning any ideas of delicacy. 'And it just might *be* yours, Riley.'

It wiped away the bass player's smirk and he made himself scarce. Nothing like paternity to spoil a good joke.

Riley stood up in stages, flexing his shoulders and back again.

'Okay, you've got my attention,' he said. 'I know I'm not the father of your baby, so what's this about?'

He unreeled to well over six feet. Annoyed by this unexpected height, Alexandra looked down to fumble a tissue from her pocket. It was too warm in here. Her glasses had fogged up and perspiration had broken out on her brow. Histamine raced through her bloodstream, puffing her eyes, stimulating the production of amazing amounts of fluid. She dabbed at it.

'Oh, God, she's going to cry,' he said under his breath. 'Come on.' He grasped her arm and towed her through the fog of smoke into a small office with comparatively unpolluted air.

'Spare me the tears,' he said in a bored tone.

'I'm not crying,' she snapped. 'But I have every right to. When I arrived home tonight there was a baby on my doorstep.'

He gave a snort of amusement. Alexandra glowered. 'Yes, hilarious. So clichéd. But it happened. There was a note with the child.' She handed the two fragments to him. 'Must you smoke in here?'

He ignored that, set the cigarette to his lips and sat on the edge of the desk, angling the paper fragments toward the light. Alexandra studied him while he studied the note. There were circles under his eyes and he was overdue for a shave. His white shirt was open at the neck, the sleeves rolled up to his elbows. Over it he wore an unbuttoned vest that matched his trousers. The clothes looked expensive and so did the gold watch he wore on a wide leather band.

He raised squinted eyes from the note. Smoke curled from the cigarette still clamped in the corner of his mouth. 'You're Miss Page, I take it?'

'That's right.'

'If the writer knows who you are—you must surely know her.'

She shook her head.

'What does it mean—"saved those other children"?'

'Never mind that. The point is, your name and this place is mentioned. If she is as desperate as she says, it seems likely that she might quote the name of the father of her child. Is that you?'

'Come on, Miss Page,' he chided. His mouth curved a fraction. 'A baby on a doorstep…a dramatic note, torn in two, tucked into its swaddling cloth… "I'm desperate and out of my mind." Very novel,' he said from one corner of his mouth. In the other corner, the cigarette bounced up and down with the words. Alexandra gave an exclamation, stepped forward to pluck it from his mouth.

Riley's dark brows shot up, dragging his eyes open wide in surprise. Deep blue eyes. Maybe a shade darker than those of the baby's. Alexandra mashed out the stub in an overflowing ashtray, then snatched up a waste-bin and tipped the mess into it.

'A non-smoker?' he drawled. 'Or just houseproud?'

She turned to him. 'I dislike mess. I dislike having my life turned upside down. I hate places like this and wild horses wouldn't drag me here normally but a baby dumped under my stairs is a very motivating force. So would you please stop being witty for a moment and apply your mind to this problem we've got.'

A wary expression appeared in his eyes and he held up both hands. 'Oh, no. *We* have no problem, lady. It's your problem and yours alone if you've found a baby on your doorstep *or* under your stairs. You need more work on your consistency, by the way.'

'But—your name is on the note!' Alexandra stabbed an index finger several times at the paper fragments.

His eyes narrowed. 'I haven't fathered any children in the past and will not father any in the future. Your alleged foundling is nothing to do with me.'

Alleged foundling? Alexandra gaped. It had never occurred to her that the man wouldn't believe her. 'Why on earth would I seek you out with a story like this, if it weren't true?'

'Miss Page, nothing people do surprises me anymore.' And indeed he had a jaundiced look about him that suggested he'd seen it all. He dropped the two fragments of the note into her hand. 'If your story is true, it's your problem. If it's not, I admit it makes a great attention grabber,' he said, with a mocking little inclination of his head.

'But—'

'Call me old-fashioned,' he went on, impressing his voice over hers without even raising the volume. 'But I prefer to be the pursuer, not the pursued, and I have to tell you frankly, you're not my type.'

He glanced disparagingly at her scarf headband and the cut-for-comfort shapeless clothes.

Alexandra's irritated eyes welled again and he must have mistaken the moisture for tears because he sighed and gave a consolatory pat to her shoulder. He thought she was crying over his brutal rejection of her sex appeal, the conceited oaf.

'Go home,' he said, and turned to the door. Alexandra grabbed his arm.

'You can't leave me to figure this out alone.'

He looked piercingly at her, his certainty wavering.

'It wasn't just *my* name on the note!' She waved it under his nose and saw that she'd been mistaken about his certainty.

'Beat it,' he said, then opened the door and walked out.

She followed but a genuine fan, blond and statuesque, slipped in beside him and put her arm around his waist. Riley grinned down at her. Plainly he didn't mind this kind of pursuit. He didn't look around again and once he sat at the keyboard he was beyond reach in his own private world.

Alexandra felt a savage thrust of envy. Fine for him, but *she* was stuck with a homeless infant and no clues. Dabbing at her watering eyes, Alexandra found a phone and rang Sam.

'No luck with Riley,' she said. 'He's used to women trying all kinds of gimmicks to get his attention and isn't convinced there really *is* a baby. I suppose there's an outside chance he's *not* the Riley on the note.' After a glum silence, she said, 'How's the baby?'

'She's sound asleep. I rigged up some divan cushions on the floor for her, and hauled up a few boxes of your books from down under to fence her in, stop her rolling off. Will you ring the police then, or will I?'

'Let me try again to get some sense out of Riley. I think he might have been starting to believe me. Can you stay on there, Sam? I might have to wait around until he finishes playing.'

She had to wait two hours. In that time, she asked around about any other club regulars called Riley but no one knew any but the pianist. She learned that he was one of the musicians who played here on amateur nights. And she learned that Riley was a first, not a last name. His full name was Riley Templeton.

She consulted the note again and decided that the torn-off word following the name 'Riley' had left behind a stroke that was almost certainly the top of a 'T' for Templeton. The smoke and noise drove Alexandra outside into a light rain.

At least the air was comparatively cool and smoke-free and her eyes had stopped watering and her nose cleared, but her singlet and shirt were wet through and clinging transparently to her skin. The scarf dripped into her eyes and reluctantly she unwound it. Her hair escaped outward and upward.

Riley emerged alone, with a leather briefcase and a jacket slung over his shoulder. He checked the oncoming traffic and strode briskly away from the club entrance to stop in front of a shopfront with a flashing neon sign. Alexandra followed.

'You again!' His eyes narrowed as if he was struck by a sudden suspicion. He glanced all around and relaxed a bit, then dropped his briefcase, pulled on his jacket, and fastened the top buttons of his shirt. 'Is this on the level—the baby on the doorstep or under the stairs? Which is it?'

'Both,' she said, with new hope and a feeling of obligation to be exact. 'My house is an old, high-set Queenslander, with a room built in down-under. The baby was left at the downstairs door, underneath the stairs that go up to the veranda.'

He regarded her with a jaded eye. 'A simple "on" or "under" would have sufficed.'

Patting his suit pockets he located a silk tie and drew it out. He scanned the traffic as he turned up his shirt collar, set the tie in position and automatically levelled and knotted it. One end of the tie flipped over his shoulder.

Alexandra's eyes were drawn to the movements of his hands and, annoyed at herself, she removed her glasses and used a tissue to wipe raindrops from them. When she looked up, he was turning down his shirt collar and making those small side-to-side jerks of neck and jaw that went with the male business of dressing.

He paused for a second as his eyes met hers, then went on to give the silk knot one last series of tweaks before he smoothed his shirt and buttoned the waistcoat. The man was so busy getting dressed that she might have to offer to give him a shoeshine to get his attention. But he certainly knew he had hers.

'What do you think?' he said sardonically, to show that he knew. Probably thought she was admiring him. She remembered his assessment of her sex appeal and resentment got the better of her.

'I was wondering if she took the nose into consideration.'

'What?' He blinked. 'Who?'

'That woman who wanted you to father a child prodigy with her.' Alexandra looked disparagingly at his nose until he raised his hand to it as if to protect it from her censorious gaze.

Then he laughed. In her limited experience, many big,

striking, confident men took themselves far too seriously but this one's sense of humour ran to laughing at himself. On the other hand, he might be so damned sure of himself that he thought it laughable that any woman might find fault with his nose or anything else.

Alexandra put her glasses on again, conscious that her liberated hair and her soaked shirt were under some intense scrutiny. With his attention firmly caught, she raised her hand in which she held the note fragments, now damp and worse for wear.

Riley showed his teeth. 'Will you stop brandishing that bit of paper at me?'

'But—your *name*—'

'Is on it. So you keep telling me!'

'Please *think* about who the writer of this note might be.'

She waved the note again and his nostrils flared, possibly from anger or possibly because he'd got a whiff of baby wee. He took a green comb from a pocket.

'I don't *need* to think about it. It has nothing to do with me and I *wish*,' he said, pointing the comb at her, 'you would stop trying to get me involved.' A gust of wind flapped his clothes and he shoved the comb between his teeth while he buttoned his waistcoat and continued to enunciate around the plastic. 'I thought the club was the one place I wouldn't be bothered by meddlesome, persistent, bloody-minded women. I've had it up to *here* with you all!'

He made a gesture at the general level of his chin, and fastened one last button.

'What—up to your comb?' said Alexandra, all mock sympathy. 'You *must* be fed up.'

He snatched the green comb from his lips. His hostility crumbled around the edges, reluctantly, she thought, as the corners of his mouth twitched into a smile.

'Take my advice. Don't get involved.'

'I *am* involved. The mother of that child didn't just abandon her anywhere. She put *my* name on the letter, asked *me* to look out for her baby in touching faith that I'm somehow the right person to turn to in her desperation, and I don't know about you, Mr. Riley, but I can't just ignore a plea like that!'

She remembered then that his last name was Templeton, not Riley, but he made no attempt to correct her mistake, just regarded her speculatively. Light rain fell. Accumulated moisture had formed a drop on the hair that hung over one of his eyebrows. She watched it slide slowly down and tremble at the extreme point.

What had she been saying? It seemed important to break the silence before that droplet fell.

'Think about it,' she said in a rush, thrusting the ragged note into her bag to fumble for a business card. 'I'll give you my phone number in case you remember something that would enable me to return the baby without a fuss if this is just a question of—of—post-natal depression or something. The authorities take a dim view of mothers who leave their infants and she might end up being supervised—'

The drop fell into the thicket of his eyebrow. God, but his eyes were so blue, his lashes so thickly black.

'—um, by a social worker—not an ideal start to motherhood. She's probably very young, by the look of the writing. Scared, I think. Can you remember a pregnant girl at the club in the last year?'

She flicked her head to stop water dripping down behind her glasses. Raindrops flew from her hair onto his face. He blinked, raised a hand to wipe water from his cheek. The film remaining on his skin picked up red, green, then red again from the pulsating neon sign. Riley licked a drop from his lip. Standing there in the street, in the rain, she felt intimately connected to him.

Confused, she realized that Riley's eyes were fixed on her mouth as hers were on his.

They both looked away in the same moment. Riley took a folded handkerchief from his pocket, swiped it across his face as if to undo the peculiar air of intimacy that had developed.

'No pregnant girls come to mind,' he said briskly. 'I'm sorry you've been lumbered with a baby by some irresponsible adult who isn't fit to bring up a child. I'd like to help but I have problems enough. Call the police before you find yourself in the unenviable situation of being charged with kidnapping.'

'*Kidnapping?*' she squeaked. 'But I didn't—'

'You've got someone else's child at your house—it could be misconstrued, take my word for it.' He used the comb briskly, returned it to his pocket and checked his watch then the traffic. As if finding what he was looking for, he nodded in satisfaction. 'Good luck, Miss Page, and goodbye.'

A bronze BMW sports model pulled into the kerb.

'Riley—hi,' called a woman. A slim, bangled arm emerged from the car and waved.

He groaned. 'Oh, God. Caroline,' he said under his breath, and swore. As Alexandra made to move away he grasped her elbow and said urgently, 'Stay.'

Like a command to a well-trained spaniel. She was tempted to bark in protest but a glance at Riley showed a film of moisture on his top lip that was nothing to do with rain, and she was almost sure she was picking up a faint air of panic. It was so intriguing that she stayed.

Caroline got out of the car. Sleek, ash-blond bob, kohl-rimmed, Nefertiti eyes, strapless red top, black miniskirt, big leather belt, long legs in sheer black tights. Rings and gold bangles. The *faux*-tart look. Nineteen, twenty?

Alexandra wondered what it was about this girl that had the annoyingly assured Riley rattled.

'Here are your car keys, lover.' Caroline tossed the keys, which Riley caught with his free hand. 'Your builder called on your carphone. He said he'll call back tomorrow with a report on the damage. You should move in with us, while your place is in a mess. Daddy would be delighted. And we've got heaps of room.'

Judging by the look in her eye, it was all in her bedroom. Maybe Daddy was broad-minded. *Lover?*

'Hello,' Caroline said, coolly assessing Alexandra. 'I'm Caroline Warner. You don't look like a solicitor... I thought Daddy said you were working on a case tonight, Riley?'

'We're almost finished,' Riley said, smoothly cutting in. He tossed the keys back to her. 'I'll be with you in a moment, Caroline.'

So plainly dismissed, Caroline went back to the car and leaned against it, arms crossed. Alexandra dragged jealous eyes away from that smooth, straight hair and tugged against Riley's restraining hand. He let go, but only to put his hands to her waist. 'What are you doing?' she croaked, gathered in close to him, the warmth of his hands sizzling through her wet shirt.

'Saying goodbye.'

He waited a moment, almost as if giving her the option of breaking away, but when she made no such move, he bent his head and kissed her. His lips were cool and efficient. It was a hearty kiss, the kind that would look good to a spectator, without aspiring to intimacy. Or so she thought for a full five seconds.

After that, his mouth opened on hers, softly teasing, persuasive. She felt the slide of his tongue and the taste of smoke and peppermint invaded her mouth for an instant, then it was over, terminated by the sharp slam of a car door.

Riley let her go. He smiled, very pleased with himself.

'It's a pity. Some other time it might have been fun to take this further. But in the circumstances, I don't expect to see you again. Goodbye, Alexandra.'

He picked up his briefcase and went to the car. Alexandra didn't wait to see him drive away but caught one last glimpse of him at the wheel with Caroline sulking in the passenger seat as the BMW flashed by.

Alexandra dragged a hand across her mouth. *It might have been fun to take this further.* The man was conceited and oversexed. And apparently mistaken when he'd said she was not his type. She found a fierce satisfaction in that.

At home, Sam was asleep on the sofa and the baby in her makeshift bed. *Working on a case,* Caroline had said.

She looked up Templeton in the phone book. And there he was, Riley Q. Templeton, Brstr-at-Law, Inns of Court. A barrister. No wonder she felt frustrated. The man tied people up in knots for a living.

Sam woke, heard the latest developments and went home. The screen door slapped closed and his boots clattered briefly then were silenced by wet grass. A goat bleated. The frog in the lily pond across the road croaked every nine seconds in the strict tempo it had kept up since December. Mosquitoes hovered, humming, outside the window screens. Distant tyres swished on the wet surface of the freeway.

Alexandra went to bed and no longer heard any of these familiar sounds, only a few notes of an elusive melody and the quick breathing of the infant. One more day, Alexandra thought. She would keep the child safe one more day in case the mother came back for her. Unlikely that Riley would help now, even if he had second thoughts. She must have dropped the damned business card and Riley would not bother to look up her

phone number. If he even remembered her name.
Alexandra ran a fingertip over her lips.

I don't expect to see you again.

Well, he wouldn't, would he? He thought that *she*
thought Riley was his last name.

CHAPTER TWO

THE case was won, but Riley was in a black mood. The details of the prosecution case he had presented were unpalatable, but pallid compared to the many others, both defence and prosecution, stored in the horror chambers of his memory.

The vague depression that hung over him was shot through with reminders of last night. He made some small talk about cases and the humidity to colleagues in the elevator of the Inns of Court and got off at his floor. His weekly escapes to play at the club revived him, especially since that other business had started. And since his mother had renewed her interest in his professional and private life.

But only a few impressions lingered from last night. Alexandra Page kissing him and exuding some scent he knew he ought to recognise but didn't. Alexandra Page waving that note in his face. And Alexandra Page shrugging her shoulders at his playing.

Riley gave a self-deprecating smile. He really must be slipping if he gave a damn whether or not he'd impressed a freckled girl with glasses and bricklayer's boots.

By now she would have given up the baby to the authorities, which was the only sensible course of action. Riley nevertheless felt a twinge of conscience. What if it *was* his name on the damned note? He flicked open his briefcase and drew out the card he had salvaged last night from the wet pavement.

Volumes—Second-hand and Antiquarian books, Memorabilia. Elizabeth Arcade.

Perhaps, if she still seemed interesting by the end of the day, and he could find the time, he might drop in at her bookshop and find out what had happened. Even ask her out to dinner if the idea still seemed amusing. He slipped the card into his pocket. Then again, he might not. She was the intense type who got involved and God knew he didn't need another female making waves in his life right now. His 'temporary secretary' and Caroline were trouble enough.

His stride checked as, through the canes of a potted stand of bamboo, he saw his secretary, a security officer and a visitor who was plainly out of place. Over one shoulder the visitor had a large, quilted fabric bag. Over the other she had a baby.

Alexandra Page. The woman's reddish-brown hair was tied back with a fuzz of curls around the hairline. She wore another set of baggy clothes and the baby was swathed in checkered towelling and some diaphanous material that trailed on the Chinese rug and was caught up now and then in an absent, winding movement of Alexandra Page's hand.

In that same hand she held a clear plastic envelope with an irregular-shaped sheet of paper inside. Riley experienced a powerful surge of anger, dislike, attraction, and a frustrated sense of having lost the initiative.

The Inns of Court repelled outsiders with its expensive, clubbish silence, the haughty quirk of secretarial eyebrows. Barristers who had their chambers here advertised their success and their taste in splendidly furnished reception areas, paintings and spotlit sculptures. In such an unreal place everything was rare and real—real leather, real marble, real silk, rare silence, original art. It was the kind of privileged place where you longed to know someone, to see a familiar face.

At least that was what Alexandra thought until she saw a familiar face.

A bewigged Riley Templeton checked at the sight of her, then bore down like a caped avenger from another century. Dark, judicial robes flared over a black, silk vest and pin-striped trousers. His eyes and brows were made darkly dominant by the framing of the silver wig and the traditional high-cut, white neckcloth. Alexandra swallowed. The ancient, legal rig-out was intended to intimidate but it was overkill on Riley.

He came to a halt and pulled off his wig as his over-protective secretary quickly made known Alexandra's crimes.

She had No Appointment. She had Refused To Leave when the baby started crying and Disturbing Everyone. 'And she Tried to Get Into Your Office,' the woman finished. Alexandra supposed she'd kept the worst crime until last.

The guard, convinced by Riley's black expression that he had been too tolerant, moved to evict Alexandra. Conscious that she might only have a few seconds to achieve her aim, she thrust the baby, face forward, at Riley Templeton.

'Does she remind you of anyone?' she demanded loudly.

He flinched, glared, and Alexandra wondered if she was the only one who noticed that his dark hair, ruffled upward from the removal of the wig, looked very like the baby's upstanding dark fluff. That his navy blue eyes were almost the same colour as hers. Confronted with the scowling man at close quarters, the baby shrank back, her lips quivering.

'Riley?' said his secretary in a demanding tone un-usual in a salaried employee. 'What is this? Who is this woman? She claims to have met you last night, which I disputed because I knew you were meeting Rob Cousins about the Janowski case last night.'

Riley swore under his breath. 'It's okay, Mum. I know Miss Page. I'll deal with it.'

Mum? Well that explained the possessiveness of the woman towards Riley's office and his time. Alexandra wouldn't have thought he was the type to still have his mother hovering around. 'Is this another *pro bono* case you haven't told me about, Riley?' his mother said with a sigh.

'No, it isn't. It's—'

'Personal,' interpolated Alexandra, annoyed with the way Mrs. Templeton had said *pro bono,* as if anyone who didn't have the money to pay for her son's services could expect only charity, not respect and diplomacy.

'Personal?' Mrs. Templeton's beautiful left hand grasped at the gold chain around her throat. She sized up Alexandra and the baby yet again and liked what she saw even less than at first, if possible. She lowered her voice but her confidential tone carried quite well to Alexandra.

'You don't have time right now, Riley, for whatever this—Young Person wants. You're due in court again shortly and if you can spare any time for Personal Matters you really should return Davina's call. I told her you would phone this morning about the tickets to the CUFF fund-raiser.'

'You did what?' he snapped.

'I have your well-being at heart, Riley,' she said reproachfully.

'Mum, I *told* you not to interfere in my—'

Incredibly, a fine film of moisture appeared in Mrs. Templeton's steel-blue eyes. Casting a driven look around, Riley noticed people from nearby chambers turned curiously in their direction. He grabbed Alexandra's arm, pushed her into his office and shut the door. She had the strange impression that he wasn't so much getting her out of the way as seeking refuge himself.

It was a room with books from floor to ceiling on two walls, some deep, broad armchairs and a splendid antique desk. Swagged curtains framed a view of the city and glimpses of the Brisbane River. A large portrait of a robed, bewigged man with smiling eyes the colour of Riley's stopped her in her tracks.

'My father,' Riley said, dourly informative.

She smiled at the artist's signature, which was better than a familiar face in this stuffy place of privilege and precedent.

'You're like him.'

Riley gave a pre-lingual grunt that signified he'd been told that before.

Alexandra sniffed the air and checked the desk, the low tables and cabinets.

'No ashtrays,' she commented with relief. 'You don't smoke in here?'

'I hardly ever smoke,' he said tersely. 'Occasionally, at the club.'

'When in Rome?'

'Why the interest?'

'I'm allergic.'

'Ah. So the tears last night—?'

'Allergic reaction.'

He flung the silver wig onto a leather chesterfield and the files onto the desk.

'Nice desk.'

'It was my father's. So, you were trying to get into my office,' he said grimly. 'What for?'

'I only suggested I wait in here because the baby was crying. Your secretary—er, mother—acted as if I'd asked to have a picnic in Westminster Abbey.'

'She's not my secretary. Just filling in for three weeks

until my permanent secretary recovers from an accident.'
He looked at her with grim resignation. 'I suppose you
blabbed about meeting me in the jazz club?'

'N-o, I didn't mention the club,' she said, watching
the small signs of his relief with interest. 'Is it a secret
from everyone, or just your mother and Caroline?'

He didn't answer as he yanked off the neckcloth,
which came free with the brisk sound of parting Velcro.
It, too, was tossed onto the chesterfield.

'Well, it's none of my business if you turn from hu-
morless upholder of the law into mild-mannered Piano-
man while your womenfolk think you're working.'

She received a darkling look. Pacing, he shrugged off
the robe, threw it accurately onto an antique hatstand.
He unfastened the top two buttons of the traditional
black, silk vest that sat high to the neck over his shirt
and tie. Alexandra wondered just how many clothes he
was planning to take off.

'So,' he said sourly, coming to a stop at last to look
at the infant. 'This is the abandoned—'

Alexandra pressed the baby's cheek to her shoulder,
cupped a hand over the tiny exposed ear. 'Sssh!' she
said. 'Don't say that.'

Riley stared. 'What?'

'That's not a word a baby ought to hear,' she said,
and mouthed the word 'abandoned.'

He made a sound halfway between a snort and a
laugh. For a moment he leaned towards her and he was
close enough for her to hear his deep intake of breath.
Alexandra wondered if she smelled of sour milk. It
seemed so. One whiff and Riley was off again, pacing
the length of his bookshelves.

'How did you know where to find me? And what the
hell are you doing here whipping up a melodrama in my
chambers *and* in front of my—' He cuffed a protruding
legal volume into line with the rest and turned to point.

'*Thrusting* that child at me as if it were *mine,* and me some randy lord who's got the chambermaid pregnant and refuses to take responsibility.'

Alexandra could not decide what angered her most—his easy assumption of himself as a lord, her in the role of the chambermaid, or that magisterial index finger levelled at her.

'"That child" is a *she,*' she snapped. 'Not an *it.* And she could well be yours—she looks enough like you. Everyone must have noticed,' she added, glad to see it annoyed him.

The baby stopped crying, and gazed at Riley with the impertinence of the innocent.

'I told you,' he said, enunciating the words crisply in a low, grainy voice that must, she thought, be most effective in the courtroom. 'I have fathered no children.'

'How can you be sure?'

'You want details of my birth control methods, Miss Page?'

She flushed and he gave a tight, mocking smile. 'I practice very safe sex,' he said deliberately. Alexandra had a series of unwelcome, very unsafe images involving tousled sheets and those hands that made music and seemed always to be buttoning and unbuttoning things.

'And I am very choosy. The kind of women who appeal to me would not leave a child on a stranger's doorstep.'

'Oh?' she queried. 'You think there are only good women and bad women—and the mother of this child is automatically one of the bad ones?'

Whether it was the soothing opulence and order of his book-lined office, or the subject, Riley was subtly in control again. 'No, no, no. I don't think anything of the sort. Good women are much too uncomfortable and bad women eventually want free legal services. Fortunately, there are many delightful shades of grey in between.'

The whimpering child was mysteriously turning from a featherweight to a heavyweight on her shoulder. Alexandra repositioned the baby and raised the plastic envelope. His eyes followed it and his blood pressure appeared to rise with it.

'You've got that *bloody* note in that plastic, haven't you?' he said with hands on hips and his very good teeth set edge to edge.

'It looked like rain,' she explained.

He stared at her then laughed. What was it about some smiles that made them more compelling than others? Was it the exact ratio of teeth and gum that showed? The lines that came into play around the mouth and eyes? She felt a powerful attraction.

'I wish you would help me, Riley. I—don't think I can do this by myself.'

'What are you suggesting? That *I* help with the baby-sitting? Change nappies?' He gave a hoot of derision at the very thought.

She had never thought to ask any such help of him, only that he try to discover who the mother might be, but his lofty attitude riled her. 'Well, why not?' she said, a gleam in her eye.

He snorted. 'I'm a barrister, Miss Page. I have pressing obligations, a court appearance shortly, important work to prepare for a new case. Even if I wanted to help—and I can assure you, I do not—I couldn't.'

Frostily, she regarded him. 'I have pressing obligations, too, Mr. Templeton, *important work* and a business to run. If I can make an effort to handle this extra responsibility just for a day or two, I don't see why *you* can't.'

'I'll tell you why,' he said, showing his teeth. 'Because it is *your* decision to keep this child from the authorities.' He levelled that index finger at the baby, who began to cry. Riley looked dismayed for a moment but sliced the air with the edge of one hand. 'It has nothing to do with me.'

She raised her hand, brandishing the plastic envelope. Riley said something sharp and explicit under his breath, clamped a hand about her wrist. 'If you tell me once more that my name is on that thing—' he said, grinding his teeth.

'Well, it *is!*'

She felt the spasm in his hand. His dark blue eyes stared into hers and now his fingers moved independently as if they were trying out notes on the soft flesh of her arm. He leaned toward her and sniffed.

Rattled by this sudden closeness, she arched away. 'You're not going to start kissing me again, I hope?'

A reminiscent gleam appeared in his eyes. 'That implies it was a one-way affair.'

Alexandra told herself that she'd hardly made any move at all—well, maybe just a twitch of the lips. Perhaps just a flick of the tongue. And, all right—her hands *had* sort of clutched at his lapels and she had a vague memory of touching his hair. She made a major business of shifting the baby from one shoulder to the other.

'I never voluntarily kiss a smoker. Don't like the taste,' she said, wrinkling her nose.

'Like I said, I only smoke at the club,' he told her as if he was seriously addressing this complaint. 'Most of the time I taste like a non-smoker.'

The man was too smooth. He'd taken her own word 'taste' and turned it from the general to the particular, from passive to active. She curbed her imagination, which was in the process of exploring the business of tasting him.

Riley leaned close and sniffed again.

'What is that—perfume, or scent, or whatever it is you're wearing?'

'I don't wear perfume. I'm allergic to it.'

'You seem to be allergic to a lot of things.'

He still held her wrist and she tugged gently away lest he detect her galloping pulse. 'Smoke, perfume, dust, seafood and permanent wave solutions,' she informed him, talking too much because her pulse wasn't slowing. And, she might have added, men who made her pulse race. She had developed that little allergy years ago, by observing the heartbreak that such men could cause.

'Permanent wave solutions?' he repeated, focusing on the wildly curling strands around her forehead. 'So why use them?'

'The curl is natural,' she said with resignation.

'In that case how would you know you're allergic to the solution?'

'Because I had my hair straightened once and came out in a rash for months.'

He blinked. 'That makes no sense.'

She thought she saw the source of his puzzlement. 'You use permanent wave solution to *straighten* hair as well as curl it,' she explained.

'That's not what I meant. It makes no sense that you would want to straighten it.'

Alexandra was so surprised that she could think of nothing to say. His eyes narrowed and for a few seconds he appeared to be weighing up something. She thought he gave a slight shake of his head as he turned away.

Pulling a wallet from inside his jacket, he selected several large-denomination notes. He plucked the plastic envelope from her fingers and replaced it with the money.

'My contribution,' he said. 'Hire a baby-sitter if you won't take the proper action. Quite frankly, I think that's more than most reasonable men would do.'

'Well, I suppose you can only give what you have to give,' she said dryly, holding up the money. 'I will accept this because you can obviously afford it and I'm on a very tight budget. But I'll keep records and you'll get back every cent that I don't spend on things for the baby.'

Riley checked his watch, strode behind his desk and tossed the plastic envelope down. 'I won't require a financial report, Miss Page.' He wrenched open the battered leather briefcase, removed a wad of papers from it and shuffled a new wad in.

Alexandra stowed the money in her bag, wound up the trailing muslin she'd swathed round the baby.

Mrs. Templeton was waiting for her, or, more correctly, lying in wait. 'Miss Page,' she said, with an investigative smile. 'My apologies for being so suspicious but one really can't be too careful, especially at present when—er—um. Where exactly did you meet my son?'

Riley appeared like magic, wearing the robe, carrying the wig, neckcloth, umbrella and briefcase. He frowned repressively to remind her not to mention the jazz club.

'Oh—in my bookshop,' she said, wondering why on earth she should lie for him. 'Yes, Riley is a regular…he comes for the comics. *The Phantom*. Archie and Jughead—'

'Comics?' The word came off Mrs. Templeton's lips as if for the very first time. 'But Riley has *never* liked comics. We never had comics in the house.'

'That probably explains it,' Alexandra said. 'So many of my customers have had their comic urges repressed in childhood and now they—'

'Yes, yes, we get the picture,' said Riley, and glared when she giggled at the unwitting pun.

He gave some instructions to Mrs. Templeton who laid her hand on his sleeve and said some urgent, confidential words, which brought a twitch to his cheek. Then he seized Alexandra's arm and steered her to the elevator.

'I may just go stark raving mad in the next three weeks,' he muttered. 'And you haven't helped. Comics!' He snorted.

In the elevator he jabbed the control board then put on the wig, rebuttoned the vest and fixed the neckcloth in place. The man was in a constant state of dress or undress.

'But I have to thank you,' he said abruptly. At her querying look over the baby's head, he went on. 'For not mentioning the club.'

She shrugged her less burdened shoulder. 'I wouldn't have lied for you, but frankly, it was a pleasure to deny your mother information.'

Riley underwent a change that illustrated the maxim 'Blood is thicker than water.' 'My mother is a wonderful woman, in her own way. She does faultless paperwork and knows almost as much about the law as I do,' he said stiffly. 'She could have lived the champagne-lunch and charity-committee lifestyle but chose to work with my father as his secretary and she's been lost since he died.' He checked in the mirror wall of the elevator and plucked the neckcloth into position and went on absently, almost talking to himself now.

'He was happy to have her organise his life. Now she misses him and has all that energy and nowhere to spend it—'

Except on her son. Alexandra tried and failed to imagine Mrs. Templeton 'lost' but she liked him for his quick defence of his mother. There were men she knew who would have called a mother less intrusive than Mrs. Templeton 'the old bag' without contrition.

'How long since you lost your father?'

'Seven months.'

Her gaze rested on the ancient leather briefcase. His father's desk and maybe his father's briefcase. Had he stepped into his father's shoes?

'I'm sorry. I shouldn't have criticised your mother.'

Riley, robed and bewigged, inclined his head regally as if in acceptance of her apology and she liked him rather less again.

'Don't you feel conspicuous, swanning around in theatrical costume from eighteenth-century England?' she said when they emerged onto the street. 'Or maybe you like to be conspicuous, impressing the hell out of us ordinary people on the streets.'

'Am I impressing you?'

'The only thing you could do to impress me, Riley, is to help me find this baby's mother.'

'Seventeenth-century actually. It all started when Oliver Cromwell put King Charles on trial. Lawyers covered their heads in protest at such a—' He hesitated, choosing his words.

'*Cavalier* action?'

He laughed. 'Some judges don't insist on the wig and gown. Others won't recognize you in their courts unless you're wearing it, which is why today I'm swanning around in theatrical costume.'

A tight-packed group of people emerged from the pub on the opposite corner and Alexandra saw a hand pointed in their direction. The group directed a collective, malevolent stare across the road and she felt the force of anger almost as a physical shock. A few clenched fists were raised, mouths opened and shut and above the clamour of traffic. Alexandra thought she heard them shout 'Bastard' and several other short and pungent words.

She looked behind them and saw nothing to account for it, then moved a fraction closer to Riley, hurrying to match his stride. He appeared not to have noticed the abusive group that was separated from them, mercifully, by traffic coming off the freeway.

'Why are those people shouting at you?' she asked,

noticing that his cold aloofness was somewhat undercut by a twitch of muscle above his jaw.

'Maybe I'm impressing the hell out of them,' he said sardonically.

As she and Riley and the baby headed along George Street, the group continued to watch them but didn't follow.

'They were in court this morning,' he said, rewarding her silence with explanation. 'Family of the defendant, a nineteen-year-old kid. I was prosecuting and won the case. Their son, brother, nephew, whatever was found guilty of aggravated assault on an eighty-year-old woman.'

'And they hate *you* for that?'

'Occupational hazard. Someone always loses. Angry people lash out. Just part of the job, and as you've already remarked,' he said sourly, 'I'm well paid for my efforts.'

But, if his mother's disapproval was anything to judge by, he also was often not paid for his efforts. *Another pro bono case,* she had said.

There was more to Riley than met the eye. She glanced sideways and so much met the eye that she missed a step and stumbled on the long length of muslin trailing from the baby. She stopped to wind it up.

'What's the matter *now?*' Riley said, exasperated.

'It's not as easy as it looks,' she protested.

Riley closed his eyes for a moment then took her arm and towed her past the Law Courts buildings with their philodendrons and palm jungles, past splashing fountains to a less conspicuous spot. He dropped his briefcase and umbrella on the pavement.

'Give it here.'

'I suppose by "it," you mean the baby?' she said breathlessly and, before he could change his mind, handed the child over. He held her at arm's length, his large hands encircling the little girl's chest. Alexandra wound up the scarf and prised a pin open with her teeth, to secure it to the striped makeshift napkin that was now damp and gently steaming.

'She'll cry if you hold her like that,' Alexandra predicted. 'I daresay she doesn't feel too secure held out like a parcel with nothing but air between her and the pavement.'

But contrarily the baby gurgled, kicked her dangling legs, slapped her tiny uncoordinated hands against his large ones, and seemed to feel perfectly secure. She stared wide-eyed at Riley and regurgitated milk over his thumb. He sighed.

'Aren't you finished yet? And why wrap it in *this* abomination?'

'Look, I'm a single bookseller—do you imagine I keep baby clothes just on the off-chance that someone leaves an infant on my doorstep? It's all I could find. My mother gave it to me, to tie up the grapevine,' she explained as the baby changed hands yet again.

'Grapevine?' he repeated, and again there was one of those pauses when Alexandra imagined he was carefully weighing things up before proceeding. At any rate, he shook his head as if deciding not to pursue the matter of the grapevine. 'Doesn't *she* have any proper baby clothes stashed away, for sentimental reasons?'

Alexandra laughed. 'My mother isn't sentimental about keeping baby clothes. She's not all that keen on babies, to be honest. She'd rather paint pictures.'

'Does that mean she won't baby-sit?'

'Well, she might do the odd hour. I'll phone her when I get to the shop.' As if in protest at being farmed out to an unsentimental painter, the baby began to grizzle. 'Oh, don't cry,' Alexandra said, jogging the child on her hip and brightly looking around for a distraction. 'Look, what's *this?*' she said to the baby in a Playschool kind of voice as she walked on toward the intersection where a bronze statue of a goddess in a spiked crown solemnly held aloft the scales of justice. 'It's a statue of Themis, Greek goddess of justice, sweetheart,' Alexandra said, reading from the plaque.

Riley gave a snort, checked his watch. 'Goodbye.'

'Oh, darn,' she said, looking up, then meaningfully at the umbrella he held. 'It's starting to rain.'

'You'd better hurry then,' he said, unmoved.

'There's *two* of us to keep dry.'

He took a deep breath, shook and flicked open the umbrella and handed it to her with an air of finality. This, his expression seemed to say, was the last thing he was prepared to do for her. He picked up the briefcase just as two police officers in uniform came past. They nodded to Riley and slowed down.

'Hand that child over to the authorities,' he advised. His eyes flicked over her clothes and he added, as an afterthought, 'Keep the money, anyway.'

He turned back the way he had come and in long strides caught up with the policemen.

Keep the money anyway... Another pro bono case. Alexandra fumed. In a clear, carrying voice she said to the baby, 'Wave goodbye to Daddy.'

She fancied that Riley's stride checked momentarily. One of the policemen looked back curiously at her and she hurried away to press the pedestrian button at the traffic lights. Was Riley even now reporting the abandoned baby to the authorities as he so strenuously advised?

Rain pelted down. Sheltering with the baby under his umbrella, Alexandra watched Riley run for cover into the courts building. There was some justice, after all.

CHAPTER THREE

VOLUMES Bookshop occupied a cramped upstairs and downstairs space in an arcade that smelled permanently of incense and took its pace from the New Age music playing in several shops. Just one street away from Brisbane's main shopping mall, it was another world of batik and dragons, adult lingerie and 'marital aids,' crystals and wholefoods, candles and copper jewellery.

Most customers were city day-trippers with time to spare, and though the career men and women who used the arcade as a short cut might look sideways at the curtained windows of the adult lingerie shop or one of the antique bookshops, all except the vegetarian and sushi diners tended to pass straight through.

So Alexandra was surprised when she was summoned downstairs by the tinkling of the bell on the door at five-fifteen, to glimpse charcoal suiting through the treads of her spiral staircase. Pin-striped and expensive, the kind she would expect to find further up the street in the large, air-conditioned, carpeted bookstore with its own coffee shop.

Volumes had no air-conditioning, no carpet and an electric kettle and an assortment of mugs for customers willing to make their own tea or coffee. This particular customer, having rung the bell, was spooning instant coffee into a mug. Alexandra heaved the several books she carried into the crook of her arm and raised her voice over the cheap roar of the kettle.

'Good evening. How may I—' Her feet slowed on the last treads and she peered through the staircase metal fretwork, recognising a certain familiar line to that back, those wide shoulders and that dark, pin-striped suiting. His dark hair was precise across the back of his neck. There were a few raindrops glistening on his shoulders. 'Oh. Riley.'

Riley raised the coffee mug from which steam issued. 'Any milk?'

'Under Romance.'

His brows went up, and she pointed. He crouched down to the bar fridge nestled under shelves of romance novels and moved a half dozen eggs to extract a carton of milk. Standing, he cast a jaundiced eye over several book covers featuring pretty women in the arms of lean, compelling, sardonic men.

Riley sipped at the coffee. He pulled a face, turned the tin of coffee powder toward him to eye the cheap brand.

'I keep the coffee for *customers,*' she said, annoyed at his unspoken criticism.

Another sip, another wince. 'And do they come back?'

'Almost without fail.'

'Your books must be good.'

He allowed himself a small smile to mark this bit of wit.

'What do you keep the eggs for? And why are they labelled "Mr. Hawkins"?'

Alexandra didn't answer as she wondered how to proceed. The man might have decided to help after all. What other reason could he have for being here, having made his goodbyes so very final—again—this morning?

Her heart slammed out a few beats as one reason occurred. Hold on, she told herself. You are not the kind of woman who has men running after them. Riley is not the kind of man to run. 'I suppose you've come for your umbrella,' she said.

He smiled and wandered over to the shelves stacked

with comic books. 'Ah. *The Phantom,*' he said, picking up one. 'The last time I read one of these I was a nerdy, scrawny sixteen.'

'Your mother said comics weren't allowed in the house.'

'Depends how you define "house." I decided my mother didn't include the cellar. Only my father ever went down to put more wine in, or take a bottle out. I spent many happy hours with a torch, my comic collection and fifteen dozen bottles of wine.'

'So why did you give it up at sixteen?'

'I grew six inches in a year, filled out, my voice finished breaking, I had the braces taken off my teeth and I could say my esses again, which was a real break because the girls I fancied all had names I hadn't been game to even say. Cassandra. Suzanne. Vanessa.' His grin widened nostalgically with each name.

Riley returned the comic to the pile and went to the shelves of antique books.

'If you're a collector of old books,' she said hopefully, when she'd given up trying to envisage him as a teenage nerd, 'I've got a very nice edition published in 1882, gold leaf on the cover, in excellent condition—it would look great with the collection in your office.' She prised it from the shelf and offered it.

'*Sermons by the Rev. W. Morley Punshon,*' he read, and gave it back with a grin. 'Trying to unload a bad buy?'

She shrugged. 'I don't think I'll ever sell it,' she said with a sigh, and reshelved it.

'Got anything on jazz?'

'There is one title in the Biography section, I seem to remember, about Stephane Grappelli and Django Reinhardt,' she said, overtaking him briskly. She hefted her burden of books into the crook of one arm and picked a volume from the shelf.

She turned to find Riley right behind her, looking over her shoulder. 'And I have a jazz magazine in good condition, dated 1937, if you're into collecting memorabilia.'

Riley braced one long arm against the shelves and leaned down to study the book. Alexandra felt the ebb and flow of his breath on her cheek. She was trapped in a dead end between Biography, Religion and Military History and wondered why she'd never before noticed how narrow the aisle was. Overhead, a ceiling fan barely stirred the air. It was quiet.

'So, where's the baby?'

Just for the moment she had genuinely forgotten the baby, distracted as she was with the faint lime fragrance he exuded and the subtle smell of the superfine fabric that clothed the arm that barred her way. And the three— no, four—blunt, straight hairs that clung to his whiter-than-white shirt collar. The man had found time for a haircut on the way here. Had he been sitting in the barber's chair when he decided to come here to once and for all get her 'out of his hair' to avoid any more scenes in his hallowed chambers?

'Actually, everything has been resolved,' she said, making the decision herself. It seemed suddenly not only a good idea to be rid of Riley, but that *she* should be the one who initiated the break. 'I came back from your chambers and an hour later, the baby's mother turned up.' Alexandra closed the book and turned with a smile. 'Isn't that good?'

Riley's blue eyes were bland and unblinking. 'Really? So what's her name?'

The fan whirled a couple of times. Alexandra swallowed. The title of a book about Lourdes caught her eye. 'Bernadette,' she said, certain he hadn't noticed her hesitation.

'Bernadette what?'

'Um—Saint, St. John.' She raised her eyebrows and gave a few signs that she would like to get past, but rather than move back, he moved forward to take the jazz book from her. There was nowhere else to go so she pressed a little harder against Military History.

'And did she tell you why she dumped her child on your doorstep?' he asked, letting the page edges riffle past his thumb with a soft, sly sound.

'Um—she—er—' The strain of prevarication was too much so she went on the attack instead.

'Look, what do you care? You've made it quite clear that you don't want to be involved, so I'd appreciate it if you didn't cross-examine me. Everything is back to normal. You won't be inconvenienced or *involved*. I'm sorry if you found it embarrassing to be confronted with a baby in your chambers but it won't happen again. I don't need your help now and—I'll give you your money back because I won't need that, either.'

She paused, slowed her breathing, feeling better now that she had cut loose from Riley Templeton. 'Do you want to see that magazine before you go?'

Still, the infuriating man didn't move out of her way. He stared at her, then reached out to touch the hair at the back of her head, where she had reknotted it using copious amounts of hair spray to tame the kinks. The faint wrinkling of his nose was reminiscent of his distaste over the cheap coffee.

'What did you do to it?' he asked. 'Last night, it was soft to touch—'

Vividly, she recalled the momentary thrust of his fingers in her hair as he kissed her. 'Would you move, please, Riley? If you're looking for a little dalliance as a diversion from work, you're in the wrong place. I appreciate being used as therapy today just as little as I appreciated being used last night. I'm not quite sure whether you kissed me to make Nefertiti jealous, or to discourage her, but either way, you had a nerve.'

'*Dalliance?*' he repeated. 'You must have a large Jane Austen section.'

'It's closing time soon. I have things to do, so goodbye, Riley. We have no need to see each other again now that mother and baby are reunited.'

'I'm not so sure about that.'

Alexandra blinked guiltily. 'Well, of course they are.'

'I meant—I'm not so sure we have no need to see each other again,' he said. 'It could be interesting. Have dinner with me.'

Her heart thumped in time with the fan revolutions, surely too slow to sustain life. Interesting? Was dynamite interesting? Was a sabre-toothed tiger interesting?

She shrugged. 'I don't think so.'

His eyes flickered. 'We have some kind of chemistry going.'

'That's *why* I don't think it's a good idea,' she said. 'Chemistry is so misleading.'

Oh, blast. The man wore a smirk now that he'd manoeuvred her into admitting to mutual attraction. 'We've got nothing else—I mean, nothing in common, not even an abandoned baby, now that she's back with her mother.'

'Ah, yes,' he said, inching the book on Lourdes forward on the shelf to idly glance at the cover. 'The baby and Bernadette St. John, reunited. Is it a miracle, do you think?'

Alexandra sighed. She should have known he would be too sharp to be taken in with such a feeble fabrication.

'It's part of my job to read faces,' he said. 'Besides, there is more concrete evidence.' He withdrew one of the books from the several still tucked under her arm. There were bookmarks bearing the *Volumes* logo inserted in each of them. 'How come you didn't call your shop *Pages Bookshop?*' he said, turning the book over.

'Someone already had registered the name,' she said shortly.

'*Care of the Infant,*' he read out loud. 'As a bookseller, I suppose you can put your hand on a book for every occasion.' One by one, he extracted the other books she held.

'*The Child to Age Five,*' he said, flipping it open to the bookmark and a diagram demonstrating the correct way to hold an infant in a bath. He closed it, shuffled another on top.

'*Three Thousand Names for Baby. Baby and You* and—hmmm, you might want to reconsider this one. My sister tells me Dr. Spock's theories fell from favour long ago.'

The door opened and the bell tinkled. A very thin, very bent old man shuffled in and doffed his Diet Pepsi cap to Alexandra.

'Mr. Hawkins,' she said, smiling. 'I've brought down a selection of my latest book lot for you to look through. And I hope you can use some eggs. My hens are laying them faster than I can eat.'

'You always say that, my dear,' said Mr. Hawkins with a wry smile. 'They would be most welcome.'

'Cup of tea?' Alexandra said.

The old man replied as always, 'Now, I don't mind if I do.'

Mr. Hawkins made his way slowly to a chair under the stairs and began sorting through a box of books. Alexandra put the kettle on, opened a packet of biscuits, took milk and the eggs from the refrigerator, conscious of Riley watching. When she turned she saw that he wore that careful, considering look that was already becoming familiar.

'So where is it?' he asked again when Mr. Hawkins had his tea. 'The baby?'

'With my mother,' she admitted with a sigh. 'I'm going to pick her up when I close the shop.'

'I'll drive you,' he said to her astonishment. 'Be on the corner of Elizabeth and George in—' he consulted his watch '—twenty-five minutes and I'll pick you up.'

'But why would you do that?'

'I had a look through my files. There is one ex-client of mine who might possibly be the child's mother. We'll collect it from your mother and go straight to her address.'

Alexandra seized his arm, gave it a little shake. 'Oh, Riley, that's fantastic! Why on earth didn't you say so right away?' She gave him her brilliant smile, warming to him now that he had stirred himself to go through his records, however reluctantly.

'Don't keep me waiting,' he said, transferring the child-care books to her. 'It's peak hour and I won't be able to stop.'

He was gone before she could press him for further details of this ex-client. Twenty minutes later, having seen Mr. Hawkins off with two westerns, a Dick Francis and half a dozen eggs, she flipped the door sign from Open to Closed.

The bronze BMW sports model was low and bore the most obvious hallmarks of expense—quietness and wide seats. Riley had an enhanced sense of the value of his own time and drove assertively, finding gaps in the peak-hour traffic which he claimed with dizzying speed.

Already on edge, she found the swerving surges and subsequent sudden braking got on her nerves.

'So,' she said, 'this ex-client of yours. What makes you think she might be the baby's mother?'

'That I can't tell you. Client confidentiality.'

'Fair enough,' Alexandra said mildly. 'What's her name?'

'You don't need to know that, either.'

'Shall I have to put on a blindfold as we approach Madam X's house?' she said tartly.

Riley laughed. 'What made you pretend that the baby's mother had turned up?'

She could hardly tell him the truth. That she felt the need to distance herself because he upset her equilibrium. That she couldn't get his song out of her head.

'Well, I felt a bit guilty, to be honest, about pestering you, getting you involved in something you hated. It seemed like a good idea to give you an honourable way out.'

He laughed softly. 'Have you ever noticed how often people use that phrase 'to be honest' when they are about to lie through their teeth?' He glanced at her. 'I think you're one of those women who dodges excitement, settles for the safe and predictable. You wanted to get rid of me.'

'That's a bit self-serving, isn't it? You're so exciting that you're too much for little, old, boring me?' She hooted. But that 'safe and predictable' rankled, all the same. In her family, where brilliance and impetuosity and risk-taking were commonplace, Alexandra was all too aware of her own ordinariness.

Riley annexed a space and trod on the brakes as he pulled in hard behind another vehicle.

'If this former client doesn't turn out to be the mother—do you have any other leads? I mean, you're *sure* whoever wrote that note isn't someone you've been—er—intimate with?'

'Certain.'

Again, there was that grim finality in the word that made her search his features for enlightenment. Surely only a monk could be so sure. But there was the heat he could casually generate, that midnight voice, the experienced kiss. Oh, no, Riley Templeton had probably not been into self-denial since he got his braces off and could say his 'esses.' Alexandra suppressed a snort of laughter, which attracted his attention.

'You must have discovered a one-hundred-percent-safe method of contraception then,' she said dryly. 'The only other way you could be so sure is if you were celibate. Or impotent. Or sterile.'

The steering wheel twitched and the car responded superbly with a quiver to the left, then the right, as Riley corrected.

'Bloody hell!' he said, throwing her an astonished look. 'Are you always so frank?'

'No, but you tend to dispense with some of the niceties when you find a baby under your front stairs. And you have to admit, it's unusual to be so adamant about something like that. Most men would at least have to stop and wonder if it were possible they might have fathered a child without knowing.'

'You'd like that, wouldn't you?' he said. 'If you could pin me down as the baby's father, you could dump it on me!'

'If you *were* the father, she—not *it*—would be your responsibility!' she retorted.

'I'm not, so it isn't.'

His terse response aggravated her already uncertain temper. 'Well, let's see—marvellous as science is, I don't believe there *is* a one-hundred-percent-sure contraceptive method…and as it seems obvious that you're *not* living a celibate existence… That only leaves one reason you can be so darned sure…oh,' she said, seeing where temper had taken her.

Sterility or impotence. And he had been so very certain. Something he'd said last night suddenly came back to her. *No can do,* he'd said to the woman who'd wanted his baby. *I practise very safe sex.*

The bronze car made the kind of sideways dive that a leopard makes to bring down its kill. Alexandra fell against the door, then back past the centre line of the car so that she brushed shoulders with Riley. 'I—er—sorry,' she said. 'That was insensitive of me—if there is some problem, I mean—'

'No problem,' he said curtly. 'And if there was, one doesn't necessarily lead to the other.'

Obviously he was saying that sterility didn't mean impotence. Male pride had to make it known that he could make love even if he couldn't make children. Alexandra felt a pang of pain on his behalf. 'I mean, I should have realized. You did say, right from the first, that you had no children and never would have, and I—oh, damn! I should have held my tongue. Riley, I'm really sorry!'

The car came to halt in the traffic and he looked curiously at her. 'So much sympathy,' he remarked. 'It's quite out of place, I assure you.'

'Oh, but—not to have your own children, ever—'

'Would that seem so terrible to you?'

'I've never even considered it. I've always assumed I would have three children, maybe four, eventually. A family of my own.'

'What if you find you can't?'

Alexandra stared at him. Confronted by the reality of someone so apparently hale and hearty who couldn't, it seemed for the first time a possibility. She shivered.

'I'd be devastated,' she said quietly, filled with compassion for him.

Riley resumed his hunt for space through the traffic.

'You have no need to waste your sympathy on me. Fertility is irrelevant to my decision not to procreate.'

Lord, she thought. Was it possible to talk about such a subject in these terms?

'There might be fewer tragedies if more people found themselves sterile,' Riley went on unemotionally. 'People who promise to love and honour and cherish and end up hating each other. I spent my first professional years in family law and I've seen too many bewildered little kids biting their fingernails while their loving parents malign each other and squabble over who'll get the three-piece lounge suite, the video recorder and the kids.'

The car negotiated another swooping change of lane. 'There are enough unhappy children in the world. Whether I'm able to have children or not is irrelevant. I won't be adding to their number.'

She felt more and more sympathetic. Riley might appear cold and academic about his incapacity, but a bitter note had found its way into his voice. As for not *wanting* to have children, she supposed that was his way of consoling himself. Riley had convinced himself that his inability was almost a public service in a crowded, imperfect world.

'And what about your plans for a large family—is there a prospective father in the picture?' he asked mockingly.

'Possibly,' she said, because he was clearly expecting a 'no' and because she felt, more than ever, that she must distance herself from Riley. 'It's too soon to be sure.'

A few moments of silence. 'What's his name?'

What *was* his name? There was no such candidate and she hadn't expected to have to enlarge on the theme.

'Graham Foster,' she said at last, learning from her earlier mistake. When telling lies, keep them as close to the truth as possible. Unlike Bernadette St. John, Graham Foster did at least exist.

'We've only been out a few times yet.' True. 'He could be very close to what I want.' False. Alexandra had already decided that a few times was quite enough, but Graham kept jogging into the shop with more of his nutty theories and more invitations.

He made a scoffing sound. 'Close to what you want? Did you write out a job description?'

'In effect,' she said, goaded by his tone. 'I decided long ago that I would choose my life partner on rational and not emotional grounds.' This was very true and urgently needed to be restated.

'*Rational* grounds—you?' Riley gave a hoot of laughter. 'I've never met anyone more likely to dive in at the deep end. You're the kind of woman who gets involved at the drop of a hat—I give you the affair of the abandoned baby as an example! Most normal people wouldn't feel obliged to do the bidding of a total stranger just because she uses your name in a note.'

'Now *that* is an exceptional case.'

'You give eggs to your underweight pensioner customers.'

She waved a hand. 'What's a few eggs?'

'And I've still to find out how you "saved those other kids,"' he said with a certain satisfaction at having made his case. 'I've never known a person more likely to get involved emotionally. The chances of you making a rational, measured decision on a husband are negligible. If I had the time and the inclination, I could prove to you how easily you could be emotionally manipulated.'

It annoyed her so much that she was encouraged to expand on her ideas, even exaggerate a little, throw in some of Graham's mad notions. Even if she never saw Riley again, she didn't want him to just slot her neatly away in some mental pigeonhole as predictably irrational.

'All the more reason I should have a plan, then.'

Riley was sardonic. 'I do hope Graham isn't a romantic.'

'No, thank goodness,' she said earnestly. 'He thinks

we're compatible and our genes would combine to create super-intelligent, super-talented offspring.' True, Graham had said just that. It was difficult to warm to a man who referred to his future children as 'offspring.'

'Graham has some—interesting theories about why people choose certain partners. Graham says the idea of romantic love has simply got in the way of basic, biological instincts.' She heard Riley's small, Gallic 'pah' and went on, expecting him to cut her down in flames at any moment. 'He might have a point, if you look at the animal kingdom. Take elk, for instance.'

Riley looked startled. 'Elk?'

'Graham says the male elk grows huge antlers not because they need them so much as to prove that they're fantastically fit and so good at finding food that they have an excess of it to put into growing uselessly huge antlers. So the females go for the biggest antlers.'

'I fail to see how that can help you in your search for the ideal mate,' Riley drawled. 'Is there a human equivalent?'

Alexandra glanced at him, wondering if he was just leading her on. He couldn't think she was serious about this rubbish, surely? 'A sports car, maybe?'

Considering that he was driving one, it was provocative. She went on. 'It's pretty useless when you think about it. Designed for speed but prevented by law from using that speed, so it only does what any ordinary car can do. But as a statement that the owner has excess money to spend on non-essentials, it's hard to beat. Graham says that's why so many women go for men in sports cars—it's their biological instinct seeking out a partner who has plenty of what counts, and for humans that tends to be money.'

Riley snorted. 'The comparison won't hold up.'

'Why not?'

'You can't get antlers on hire-purchase.'

CHAPTER FOUR

LESS than five minutes from her mother's place, Alexandra stared up in horror at a giant billboard portrait, twisted in her seat to watch as they passed.

'That's Gina Esposito, the Channel Three newsreader! Hell and high water! How long has *that* been there? I hope she hasn't seen it.'

Frowning, Riley looked down at Alexandra's childishly crossed index fingers. 'Who?'

'My mother,' she said reluctantly, facing front again. 'She isn't very fond of Gina Esposito. Even a television-sized image of her is too big for my mother.'

'Not surprising. She's young, beautiful, talented, and highly paid. I daresay she brings out the worst in middle-aged mums,' said Riley.

'Well, Gina ran off with *this* middle-aged mum's husband,' snapped Alexandra, furious at his unconsciously patronising air.

'Ah. Sorry.' Riley creased his brow. 'I read something about that, surely—' But his mobile rang and he was engaged on a cryptic conversation about someone who 'had probably vented his anger now and was no longer dangerous.' He disconnected with a glance at Alexandra who feigned disinterest in the call and told him to take the next left turn.

Her mother's house was a rambling old place built at the turn of the century. The garden was a wilderness, long grass and ferns and rampant passionfruit vines presided over by palms and a mango tree heavy with late fruit. A windfall of overripe fruits were scattered on the ground, some of them half eaten by fruit bats and possums. The smell of the fermenting fruit lay heavy on the evening air and bees lingered over the golden remains, raising a lazy buzz.

The back door was open and Alexandra led the way inside. 'Rhona?' she called. They passed through into a huge studio that contrasted lavishly with the dilapidation of the rest of the house. Around the walls and on the floor were large charcoal drawings of naked figures. Half a dozen students were rolling up sketches and packing away chalks and brushes and bottles of ink. A model was unselfconsciously stepping into his undies.

Just then Rhona emerged from behind an easel. She was a tall, slim woman with a braid of dark red hair over her shoulder, a palette knife in one paint-smeared hand. Her gaze was wide and vague, as if her eyes were seeing but her brain was not processing the images.

'Rhona,' Alexandra said with the cautious sound of one speaking to a sleepwalker.

The green eyes cleared. She smiled, activating fine lines around mouth and eyes. 'Lexi—hello. How lovely to see you.'

'I was here earlier,' Alexandra said sharply. 'You do remember, I hope.'

'Of course. You left a baby with me,' her mother said.

'We've come to collect her. This is Riley.'

Her mother held her hand out to Riley, who was looking nonplussed at the actuality of this middle-aged mum.

'You're Rhona Thompson, the portrait artist. Alexandra said you painted but I had no idea…I have one of your early portraits in my offices.'

Rhona smiled the kind of smile that encouraged people to believe she was hanging on their every word. Alexandra recognized all the signs of the abstraction that came on with the incubation of another work. In consternation, she looked around for signs of the baby.

'Of my father—Gerald Templeton,' Riley went on.

'Oh, yes,' said Rhona with absent warmth. 'Temple-ton.'

'Rhona—you said you wouldn't start a new painting today because you had a class,' Alexandra complained. 'I would never have left Brenna with you if you'd told me you were starting a new work. Where is she?'

Rhona looked down at her palette knife, turned it a little to inspect the aubergine-coloured paint on it. 'Warm it up,' she muttered. 'A touch of cadmium...'

Alexandra threw up her hands and searched. 'The poor little mite is probably lost under a pile of charcoal sketches.'

But the poor little mite lay on a padded rug between some spare easels, rolling from side to side, holding her feet and gurgling as she stared up at the skylight.

'Oh, the baby—' Alexandra's mother went over and wiggled her fingers at the child who cooed and smiled and kicked her feet in delight. 'I've got your old cradle put away somewhere but couldn't find it...she was a bit grizzly after she had her milk...I wonder if cow's milk agrees with her?'

Rhona looked around with her disengaged air until her gaze held on Riley. 'You must be her father. She's very like you.'

'No,' Riley said in exasperation. He set the heel of his hand against his brow then followed through with a savage sweep of fingers through his hair, leaving it standing up and the likeness between him and the child emphasised. 'She is not mine. I have no children.' His eyes turned to the skylight. 'Why is it that I have to keep on *saying* that?'

Alexandra's mother shrugged. 'It was just the colour of your hair and the eyes—' At the flash of warning in his blue eyes, she went on soothingly, 'But it's none of my business.' Her attention sharpened on him. 'Oh, yes—Gerald Templeton. I remember your father,' she said, betraying the fact that she'd only pretended to re-member him earlier. 'There's something about the eyes…' She came over and took his chin and turned it, studied his features. 'Have you ever sat for a portrait?'

'Rhona, have you got the spare disposables I brought? Brenna needs changing.'

Her mother waved her in the general direction. 'And I put a bathtub and some washcloths with them, in case you don't find the mother. Oh, and some mangoes.'

Rhona and Riley talked together while Alexandra knelt and changed the baby. Alexandra strained to hear what they said, but as they moved to the far side of the studio all that came to her was a friendly sort of murmur.

Riley eventually returned to watch her slot the baby's legs into plastic pants.

'*Three Thousand Names for Baby* and you come up with Brenna?'

'It means "raven-haired one," and she has dark hair.'

'What's wrong with Susan or Sara?'

'Or Vanessa, or Cassandra or something else with 'ess' in it?' she said tartly. Alexandra seized the dis-carded nappy between thumb and forefinger and stood up.

'Look, I'm the one who got up to her during the night. *I'm* the one who has been changing her, feeding her and walking the floor trying to get her off to sleep. Why should *you* just stroll in and get to name her?' She thrust her face close to his. *'Brenna!'* she said.

She left the room to dispose of the nappy. When she returned, the students had gone and her mother was at her easel. Brenna still lay on her mat and Riley stood alongside taking no notice of the infant.

'Thanks for your help, Rhona.'

Her mother's sleepwalker's look was back but it faded slowly as her gaze went to Riley who appeared lost in contemplation of a painting. From the floor, Brenna looked earnestly up at him, her eyes round in fascination. Alexandra wondered what his tall, aloof figure looked like from the baby's perspective.

'Haven't seen you with a man for ages,' Rhona commented.

'He's helping me find the baby's mother, that's all,' said Alexandra.

'He's got presence. Good body. Excellent nose.'

'You make him sound like a bottle of good red wine,' Alexandra said with a giggle, and her imagination reworked some earlier fancies into scenes of wine tasting. Her mother was already sleepwalking again as she stared at Riley's profile, which tilted downward as he finally felt the pull of the baby's stare.

Brenna kicked her legs, waved her arms and made some gurgling sounds up at Riley. He bent toward her and extended a hand idly in a gesture meant to be momentary. But the baby got a grip on one of his fingers and gazed steadily up at him. There seemed almost a thread connecting them along the line of vision, and it was the man who was reeled in.

Riley knelt beside her and said something in a low voice, then tweaked her chubby body. The child gurgled, kicked the man's forearm. One tiny, bare foot vanished into the vastness of Riley's hand. And still that thread held them, in an ancient form of communication that needed no words, just the infant's trust and the man's good nature. Alexandra's stomach lurched, as if she'd suddenly experienced a change of altitude.

'He's probably calling her 'Suzanne,'' she said darkly, to dispel the unexpected magic.

Rhona turned away to the new painting on her easel as Riley joined them with the baby on his shoulder.

'Did you come along Milton Road?' she asked, applying some paint with vigour. 'Did you see the poster of your stepmama? Beautiful, isn't she? Not a line in sight. I daresay they airbrushed one or two out—she is thirty now, after all.'

'Rhona—' Alexandra was concerned by the sudden fury in the low voice. It was something that turned Rhona from time to time into an unlovely, jealous being, irrational, raging. It was one very good reason Alexandra was never going to choose a life partner on impulse, because of animal attraction, or because of some wild, romantic notion of soul mates without considering the long-term possibilities. Her mother had done it with Charles, and then Charles had gone and done it with Gina.

'Rhona—don't drive along Milton Road, please.'

The easel trembled from another jab of the paintbrush.

'I've no intention of scurrying around the backstreets because of a tasteless billboard. Anyway, Lexi, dear, I've been over it for ages,' Rhona said, and she smiled so gaily in her denial that Alexandra was alarmed. No, her mother would not drive the backstreets. She would deliberately pass the poster every day just as, Alexandra suspected, she watched the Channel Three current affairs every night, as a kind of punishment for doing whatever it was she had done to lose the love of her husband.

Rhona put down her brush and threw a cloth over her easel.

'I hope you two find this child's mother. Or father,' she said. 'Though fathers are harder to pin down, aren't they?'

'You saw that portrait in my office,' Riley said as he opened the car door for her and absently took her bag. 'Why didn't you say your mother was the artist?'

'It seemed irrelevant.' She eased backwards onto the seat, clutching Brenna to her chest.

Riley consulted a road directory.

'So, the fabulous Gina Esposito is your stepmother,' he said, tracing a long forefinger over a map.

'Actually she's not. My father—he was a sculptor—died when I was a child and Rhona married again. It's my stepfather who left to live with Gina.'

It took them half an hour to reach his ex-client's house and only minutes to find out that they were on a wild-goose chase.

'Yes?' she said through the safety chain, then recognized Riley and closed the door briefly to take off the chain. She looked curiously at Alexandra, blankly at the baby.

'Hello—I don't even know your name but I think you might know me—' Alexandra stopped as there came the sound of a baby crying from inside the house.

'Oh,' Alexandra said, deeply disappointed. 'You already *have* a baby!'

The door closed several inches. The woman looked suspicious.

Riley took Alexandra's arm in a firm grip. 'Our mistake, Ms. Marshall. Our apologies for disturbing you. Good night.'

He steered her back to the car.

'"Oh. You already *have* a baby!"' he mimicked. 'You sounded as if you were delivering babies to the door, like pizzas.'

'Sorry, sweetie,' Alexandra murmured with her cheek resting on the baby's downy head. 'I thought we'd found your mother—'

'Damn! I was counting on her being the mother. Why don't I drive you straight to a police station?'

'That's the sum of the effort you're prepared to make, is it?' Alexandra said. 'One try and you want to take the easy way out! If I can bear the inconvenience for another twenty-four hours—I don't see why you can't.' She paused a moment. 'No, that's not fair. You've done a great deal, Riley, and I'm the last person who should be lecturing on getting involved...'

Riley looked interested in pursuing this, but a thought struck her as she gazed at him. 'You realize I'm going to have to use that bath now and I've never bathed a baby in my life! Last night I just washed her all over.'

Riley took a deep breath, expelled it harshly. 'I'll take you to wherever your car is parked and you can make your own arrangements from now on, do you understand?'

Alexandra turned anxious eyes from the baby to Riley. 'What if I drop her?'

'Did you hear anything I said just now?'

'What if I get soap or shampoo in her eyes?'

'Where is your car?'

'And what I can't see is how you can successfully hold the baby upright in the water and wash between her toes at the same time.' She glanced over as Riley made a sort of 'grrrrr' sound. 'Kings Car Park.'

But in spite of his irritation, and his wish to get rid of her and Brenna, his driving was slow, careful. No lunges into a faster traffic lane, no racetrack surges to beat the amber. When a car stopped suddenly in front of them and he had to apply the brakes, Riley put out a protective arm in front of her and the baby. She smiled at him.

'You're driving like a father,' she remarked, and was instantly sorry. In spite of what he said, she was sure Riley's permanent childlessness was a sensitive area. And sure enough, his eyes narrowed and his jaw tensed.

To apologise could only make it worse. She closed her eyes. What was more surprising than Riley's new sedate driving style, was the fact that it hadn't crossed her mind to *tell* him not to drive as if he was racing in a Grand Prix. At some deep level, she must have assumed that Riley's instincts were reliable. Alexandra had a feeling she ought to examine that assumption but she was too tired. In her arms Brenna relaxed into sleep and, listening to her short, quick breaths and lulled by the comfort and low hum of the car, Alexandra, too, dozed off.

A sudden stillness woke her. Her eyelids flickered upward and she dreamily noticed that she was in her own driveway alongside Sam's plum trees. She looked over at Riley and smiled.

'Don't worry,' she said. 'I've already forgotten the name.'

'What name?'

'Ms. Marshall.'

He gave a snort that could have been amusement or exasperation and got out of the car to gather up several shopping bags from the back seat. She, too, got out, awkwardly protecting Brenna's head.

'Why have you driven me home? What am I going to do about my car?' Her attention fell on the bulging shopping bags. 'What's in the bags?'

'In the order of asking,' he said, taking her arm as they moved toward the front steps. 'One—you fell asleep. Two—the car can stay in the car park overnight. Three—bottles, baby food, nappies, vests, non-sting shampoo and um—a rattle. I stopped at a pharmacy.' He paused and looked at the door and window at ground level beneath the front steps. 'Is that where you found her?'

'Yes. The mother must have thought that was my main entrance, down under, but I hardly ever use it. Look, why are you doing this?' she asked. A rattle? He'd bought a rattle while she and Brenna had slept in his car?

'Several possibilities occur to me,' he said dryly. 'And they all rest on an impaired mental state induced by legal stress. Give me your keys.'

When she stared at him, uncomprehending, he reached inside her bag and rummaged until he withdrew a large bunch of keys. He dropped them and they fell into the herb pot.

Riley bent to retrieve them and stood up, brushed off some torn leaves and sniffed at his hand. Halfway up her front stairs he snapped his fingers.

'Basil!' he exclaimed, as if he had been handed the answer to a universal problem.

CHAPTER FIVE

'I HAVEN'T been growing herbs for long but the basil's doing particularly well,' Alexandra said, and it seemed to Riley that she was speaking faster than before.

A miscalculation had her, the carry-all and baby momentarily stuck in the doorway with him and the shopping bags. For a moment they were nose to nose and thigh to thigh. A peculiar combination of smells and scents assailed him. Basil and baby powder, sweet and sour milk, and some other fragrance that was as thready as the note of a flute behind guitar and double bass. He felt the momentary sharpness of her hipbone as she turned, followed by the evocative slide of her rounded flank, gone all too soon.

Alexandra broke free of the traffic jam.

'The rosemary is doing well, too. There's a legend about rosemary…that it never grows any higher than, oh, about 5'9", which was supposedly Christ's height. If it reaches that height it only continues growing outward, not up.'

'Is that so?' said Riley, noting with pleasure the hint of breathlessness in her voice.

'And when we say rosemary for remembrance, that's because just the fragrance was thought to sharpen the memory in ancient times. Students put rosemary leaves between their lesson book pages so that when they studied…'

Riley let the herbal lore wash over him.

He closed the screen and left the door open to let in the breeze, followed Alexandra inside, glancing around with interest at her home.

An impression of earthiness came to him, compounded of wooden floors and handmade rugs and several small, metal sculptures, of pottery and Rhona's large, honest paintings on timber walls, of sheaves of dry leaves hanging upside down from twine-bound stems. And books—on shelves, under coffee tables, on a wide windowsill, on the mantelpiece and, ironically, in the hearth of a fireplace. On a dining table, a thick book with botanical drawings of herbs lay open in pride of place on an old, carved bookstand.

There was a pattering on the roof, the sound of hesitant applause. The smell of rain wafted in through the open door. With it came the scent of the basil they had disturbed downstairs.

Basil, for God's sake. It hadn't been some evocative French perfume that had teased at him for twenty-four hours but a herb that he quite liked in scrambled eggs. Not for the first time since last night, Riley felt apprehensive. He hoisted the bags onto the table and made for the door.

'—Thyme, of course, was a herb that became very popular as a garden border in mid-Victorian times because it was low, and hardy and wasn't as easily damaged as other border plants were by crinolines sweeping past—' She turned at the sound of the opening screen door. 'Oh, Riley—please don't go!'

She was dishevelled and just a hint of panic showed in her wide, grey eyes as she stared at him over the baby's head. Instantly she regretted saying it, he could see. Alexandra Page ran her own business, seemed very self-contained in her own house and probably didn't often beg for help. He found it very attractive.

'I'm going to fetch in the bathtub,' he told her. There was an ominous familiarity about this feeling of having lost the initiative, he decided, as he ventured outside to fetch the baby's bath from his car. He had been making decisions based on irrational things like Alexandra Page clutching at his arm, giving him that warm smile of approval when he thought he'd found the child's mother. *Oh, Riley!*

You're driving like a father. That was another one. Before she'd said that, he was within minutes of delivering her and the baby to her car and kissing the whole thing goodbye. Instead of which, he was here and any kissing on his mind wasn't the goodbye kind. As he emerged from the car, carrying a baby bath full of mangoes, he stepped in a puddle and an overhanging plum tree bough dumped additional raindrops on him. He cursed roundly.

Another half hour, he'd give it. A half hour at the most. Then he was out of here.

The baby bath was on the towel-covered dining table with soap and other paraphernalia set out beside it. The baby was nakedly ready for bathing. The book of herbs had gone from the carved bookstand. It had been replaced by a baby-care volume, open at the bathing diagram.

'I thought I would just somehow *know* how to do this,' she said plaintively. 'I mean, my mother did it with her mind mostly on painting, so I just assumed it must be instinctive… Is the water too hot, do you think?' she asked with pleated brow.

With a sigh, he took off his jacket and waistcoat, rolled up his shirt sleeves and dunked an elbow in. 'I'm not screaming, so I suppose it's okay,' he said.

Brenna *was* screaming, but at the first lap of water on her feet as Alexandra cautiously lowered her, her cries grew spasmodic.

'I'll hold her, you wash,' said Riley, stepping in close beside Alexandra to replace her hands with his under the baby's arms. Alexandra grabbed soap and hurriedly lathered Brenna's toes and legs and tummy. She scooped water onto Brenna to disperse the bubbles and a miraculous silence fell, broken only by the baby's vigorous kicking and splashing.

Alexandra wiped spots off her glasses. 'She likes it, Riley.'

'I'm glad someone is enjoying it,' he said, but he was blinking drops of bathwater from his eyes and smiling, too.

'We have to wash her hair now.' Alexandra dried her hands, and turned a page to the Washing Baby's Hair diagram. She turned the bookstand so that he could see. 'Can you hold her like that?'

Riley obligingly tucked Brenna under one arm and leaned over the tub. Alexandra manoeuvred herself into position to use the shampoo and ended up tucked in against Riley's chest.

'Your shirt's wet.' She glanced up and realized just how cosy their trio was. Riley's face was spattered with drops of bathwater, his collarbones were visible through the soaked shirt fabric, his dark hair, already damp from the rain, glistened with Brenna's bathwater. And cradled in one muscular arm was tiny Brenna, gurgling, her large blue eyes fixed on him. Alexandra dragged her own eyes away.

The man definitely had sex appeal whether scruffy and unshaven in a seedy jazz club, magisterial in his judicial robes or steel-smooth in his pin-striped suit. But of all the images she'd had of him so far, she wished she could have been spared this one.

Shaken, Alexandra went to work gently but speedily with the shampoo. Brenna's hands and feet quivered with pleasure. She gurgled and drooled.

'Sheer joy,' remarked Riley, laughing. 'This is the way all kids should be, don't you think?'

'Absolutely.'

'It hurts me to think that heaps of kids in the world probably never even laugh or play,' he murmured, looking down benignly at Brenna. Alexandra's empathy was engaged. He might appear tough and cynical but Riley's heart was in the right place.

'My mother's just joined the committee of a charity called CUFF, Children Under Fire Fund. They raise funds to help kids who live in war zones—provide toys and safe places for kids to play when their neighbourhood is a mess of broken masonry and leaking pipes and exposed live wires. Some of the poor little blighters have nothing to play with but a few stones.'

'I'd like to contribute to that,' said Alexandra at once.

'You can,' he said easily. 'I have two tickets to a fund-raising dinner in March. Come with me.'

Alexandra adjusted her glasses with a foamy hand.

'I don't think so,' she said, smearing the foam over her lenses in an effort to remove it.

'You don't think it's a good cause, then?'

'Well—yes—but I'd rather make a donation.'

'How much?'

'I don't know—twenty dollars, thirty,' she said, annoyed to hear a note of apology in her voice.

'The tickets are three hundred dollars a double. If I don't have someone to partner me, I won't buy them. I think you'd have to agree that CUFF would benefit more from the ticket sales than from your twenty dollars.'

'Well—yes—'

'And you want to help.'

'Yes—'

'So I can count on you.'

'Well, yes—'

Alexandra peered up at him and wondered just what she had agreed to. The man was a menace with his quick-fire courtroom technique.

She bridled. 'Look, I didn't mean I want to go to a dinner with you.'

His smile was pure wolf. 'But you said yes anyway. Just a little demonstration of what a soft touch you are. Mention some poor little orphans and play on your emotions and—*voilà*. So tell me again,' he mocked, 'how you're going to make rational lifestyle decisions.'

Alexandra's temper fizzed. 'You really *do* like to prove your point, don't you, Riley? Can't you bear not to win an argument?'

He laughed. 'I usually do.'

'Anyway, you've only proved that I have a social conscience, that's all. Now hold her still, while I rinse this shampoo off.'

More water was flung their way during the rinsing and by the time Brenna was cosily dry, diapered and dressed, Riley and Alexandra were wetter than ever.

She lay Brenna on a rug on the floor, tossed Riley a towel and hurried to the bedroom to wrap herself into a crossover skirt and pull on a cotton-knit top. As the pleasures of the bath wore off, Brenna's hunger reasserted itself and her rising howls sent Alexandra skidding over the floor to heat milk for her feed.

She skidded right into Riley who had the towel over his head. Blindly he grabbed at it and her, and Alexandra became aware that he'd taken off his wet shirt in the instant that she touched down for support on his muscular shoulders. Seeking a safer means of support, her hands leapt from shoulders to biceps, to a broad, hairy chest and came to rest at last on some smooth, provocatively contoured expanse. For one second more she was clasped against Riley, her arms around him, her hands spread on his bare back as if that was their natural destination.

There was a low roaring in her ears.

Riley peered down at her from beneath the crooked cowl of a dark blue towel, a most unlikely monk.

'My shirt was soaked, so I took it off,' he said, rather unnecessarily she thought. Prickles of moisture broke out on her skin. This weather, she thought, was impossible. So sultry. So extraordinarily hot, even for the subtropics.

'Oh. So you have,' she said, looking at his chest as if it had only just come to her notice. She removed herself from the hot zone and continued on her way to the kitchen. Her hands tingled. And what the hell was the matter with her knees?

Riley followed her, still towelling his hair. He was barefoot. 'I put it in your clothes drier. With my socks. I stepped in a puddle.'

Of course, that sound was the drier. So much for the roaring in her ears. Alexandra felt better. She put milk on to heat and tried to ignore Riley. Why on earth had she practically begged him to stay? Now she couldn't wait to get rid of him. How long would it take his shirt to dry?

The navy blue towel was in turmoil in her peripheral vision.

Surely, she thought crossly, so many muscles didn't have to churn in order for him to dry his hair?

Surely she could have put on something more substantial, thought Riley. That thin cotton skirt was practically see-through and the top…his eyes lingered on the knitted top that kept slipping off one shoulder, then the other. Each time she hitched it back with one of those shrugs with which she'd dismissed him time and time again.

He couldn't figure her out. He was sure she was attracted to him. She'd as good as admitted it. Yet there were times when he felt she didn't give a damn about him except for what he could do to solve the baby problem. Maybe she really could override her instincts and emotions where he was concerned. Riley, who applauded rational judgment above all else, found the idea unappealing.

Alexandra delved in one of the shopping bags for the cereal baby food. One shoulder made an appearance. 'Are you sure Brenna's old enough to eat this?' she said, reading the instructions.

'The woman attendant at the chemist said it was okay.'

'But you don't know how old the baby is,' she objected. 'It says here to start giving the cereal between four and six months.'

'Look,' Riley said, 'I told the woman the baby was about this big—' He held his large hands apart, the way a fisherman did to demonstrate the size of a catch.

Alexandra laughed and gave him one of those smug, patronising looks that women kept for poor, bumbling males out of their depth. The bathtub success had gone to her head. She'd forgotten that she'd been scared stiff and as ignorant as he over the whole damned business. Riley felt that a modicum of surprise and approval might have met the thoroughness of his provisions. He was, after all, flying pretty much by the seat of his pants when it came to babies.

'Then she came and took a look through the car window to be sure. She's had four kids of her own and she assured me they all had that same cereal when they were that size and lived to healthy adolescence and beyond. Okay?'

Alexandra gave a shrug that riled him more than the 'mere male' expression. And now the cotton top was back in place and he didn't even have the compensation of that lovely, faintly freckled, bare shoulder.

Right. Well, he had done all that any decent man could be expected to. No way was he going to be suck-ered in by any more of her *Oh, Riley*s and that *I need you* expression she got in those big, grey eyes. He had to wait around now until his shirt dried, but as soon as it was ready, he was out of here. Like a shot. Twenty minutes at the outside.

Riley was sitting, shirtless, in a lounge chair, feeding Brenna her bottle when the screen door opened and slammed and Sam came in.

'Well, blow me down,' Sam said, taking a good, long look at Riley, his shirtlessness, his bare feet. Sam sent a wicked glance at Alexandra then concentrated on Riley. 'You the poor little ferret's dad? She's the spitting image of you.'

Riley's nostrils flared. Alexandra, understanding at last that his anger over these frequent allusions was based on Riley's bitter knowledge that he never could be a father, hastily cut in and introduced them.

'Riley kindly offered to give Brenna her bottle while he's waiting for his shirt to dry, so that I can make up her cereal.' She flipped a page on the baby-care book. 'Oh, damn. We should have given her the cereal first, Riley.'

'I don't think she knows that,' said Riley, glancing down at the infant who lay trustingly in the crook of his arm, her toes curling and uncurling as she sucked at the bottle.

Riley and Sam progressed rapidly to mateship. Alexandra left them to it and took the opportunity to dash outside to pick oregano and Italian parsley, to chop tomatoes for a pasta sauce for her own dinner. She was starving.

The baby finished the bottle and after only a fleeting glance at the diagram of Burping Baby open on the carved bookstand placed beside him, patted her back until she burped. He stood and transferred her to

Alexandra's arms, a manoeuvre not without a certain piquancy considering Riley's partial nudity.

'Your shirt must be dry now,' she said a bit too sharply.

'You should have said if it was disturbing you,' Riley said with a glinting look. 'I could have borrowed that shirt you had on this morning to cover up.'

He left to fetch his shirt, having delivered a double whammy; one, that he knew she was uneasy with him around bare-chested, and two, that the shirt she'd worn this morning was big and baggy enough to fit over even his broad shoulders. That she doubted, but the criticism stung. Riley was so ready with his criticisms—her coffee, her clothes, her name for the baby.

As Brenna spluttered and drooled the first of the cereal baby food, Riley and her neighbour struck up an easy exchange that required no input at all from Alexandra. The younger man pulled on his shirt and fastened the lower buttons, not before time. Now that he was more or less dressed again, Alexandra's gaze was drawn to his bare feet.

They were the intimately pale shade of feet that were perpetually shod. You could know some people a lifetime and never see their feet. Under normal circumstances she never would have seen Riley's. She'd only met him last night and already his socks were in her drier.

'Your socks must be ready now,' she said.

Riley produced a single sock. 'One has gone missing.'

'How could it?'

'Happens to me all the time. I put in pairs and get back singles. A parody of life, you might say.'

Sam snickered and, as Riley sat down to put on his shoes without socks, said, 'I went through some stuff at my place. Found an old cot my niece left here. It looks okay. Found some old 78 records I forgot about, too, and a Hornby train set must be fifty years old—'

'Seventy-eights?' Riley said, his interest quickening. 'What's on them?'

'Ellington—might be some of Errol Garner,' Sam said. 'I suppose you'd be interested, being a piano player. I've got an old Steinway, too. I play a bit now and then. It needs tuning but it's too damned expensive—'

'I could take a look at it,' offered Riley.

Alexandra sighed. 'The cot?' she said pointedly to remind them of priorities. 'What about the cot?'

'Oh, yeah. Riley and me will bring it over,' Sam said. Riley followed Sam out.

Ten minutes later, from across the paddock, came the clear piano notes of Joplin's 'The Entertainer.' A showpiece if ever there was one.

The music stopped and nothing happened for another ten minutes. They were probably playing with the train set, she thought, disgruntled. Alexandra was wiping cereal from Brenna's face, the furniture and herself, when they came back carrying the cot. Sam was telling Riley about his reunion with his army mates in Melbourne next month, as confiding as if he'd known the younger man for years. Her mother, Sam, even Brenna whom he'd referred to as 'it'—everyone took to Riley. It made her very uneasy.

They put the cot down in the living room and stood by it, as if it was a rare animal they had hunted down in the wild. Rather sourly, Alexandra wondered if they were waiting for applause.

'This bloke really *can* play piano,' Sam said, slapping Riley on the back.

'Oh, was that Riley playing?' Alexandra said, as if the polished performance could be mistaken for Sam's occasional plunkings of 'Chopsticks.' 'Your piano *does* need tuning. It sounds awful.'

It was churlish and unlike her. Sam gave a silent whistle of surprise. Riley eyed her with the kind of speculation she was sure he used on a witness who had suddenly displayed a weakness.

Brenna grizzled and coughed up some clotted milk.

'I had no idea babies needed so much *wiping,*' Alexandra said and, finding the box of tissues beside her exhausted, looked around for her bag, which contained the pile of towelling cloths from Rhona. It was Riley who found the bag and extracted a cloth, handed it to her.

Sam gave an evil grin. 'It's like watching a heartwarming TV commercial for baby powder.' When the baby began to cry in earnest, he picked up the rattle that was still in its vacuum packaging, sealed tight as any pharaoh's tomb. He gave up trying to get it out and shook it, still encased, at Brenna. 'You ought to try her on goat's milk,' he said. As the screams escalated, he showed the whites of his eyes, downed the rattle and beat a retreat.

Riley would soon follow. Rats deserting a sinking ship, thought Alexandra, feeling just a bit panicky about being left alone for another night with a fractious baby.

But Riley didn't follow. His body turned toward the front door but he looked back at Alexandra attempting to soothe the crying baby. Again she had the impression that he was weighing up the pros and cons.

To be or not to be. To stay or not to stay.

He stayed. And she was glad.

'Music,' he said, moving purposefully to her stereo. 'What have you got?' He crouched and pulled out the CD deck to check the resident discs. With a grunt, he replaced a few with new selections from her shelf, then set it to play. The rejects lay in a forlorn pile. Alexandra was dying to know which they were.

'There's a theory,' he said, coming to sit beside her on the divan. 'That music came about as a way of soothing fractious children.'

The strains of Mozart's 'The Magic Flute' overture filled the room. Brenna raised the roof. Alexandra raised a brow, said dryly, 'Really?'

Riley reached across to stroke Brenna's head. Her cries wavered, petered out. Riley's voice, low and deliberately monotonal, went on. 'Think of it—our earliest ancestors, hairy, no language—just grunts, roaming from cave to cave following some food source—carrying the babies.'

He removed his caressing hand and the almost-sleeping baby stirred and let out a few preliminary cries again. Awkwardly Riley resumed the movement, then slid his other arm around Alexandra's shoulders and tilted her toward him so that he could reach the baby's downy head that way. Alexandra would have objected but a promising silence from Brenna met this manoeuvre.

'Imagine trekking from cave to cave for days on end, with kids screaming blue murder like Brenna,' went on Riley in that hypnotic single tone.

'I'm trying not to,' Alexandra said in the same monotone. Brenna grew heavy on her shoulder as she slipped into sleep and Alexandra's supporting arm was cramped.

'So, they made sounds to them. Singsong sounds using different registers. And the human brain responds to certain combinations of sounds. That's why sudden changes of key or harmony can give you The Chill.'

A designer silence followed.

She flexed her rapidly stiffening neck and said, in the same low tone, 'I know that's my cue to ask, so I'll ask. What's "The Chill"?'

He smiled and lifted his hand a moment from Brenna to gently push Alexandra's head sideways until it rested against his. That was the second time tonight Riley had noticed what she needed and provided it.

'The Chill is that shiver down your spine, goose bumps when the music is playing on your emotions,' said Riley. 'You get it when you hear a change of key.'

Well, in the spine-shivering department, he should know, thought Alexandra. She'd always assumed that a man who just knew when you needed a washcloth to wipe the baby's face wouldn't also be the one who could send shivers down your spine. She'd always assumed that you'd have to make your choice—washcloth or shivers. But then, things being what they were, in Riley's case it was definitely the shivers. A pity really. She was beginning to think he had the makings of a super wash-cloth man.

'So—you think all this began with our Cro-Magnon ancestors?'

'And because of children. Just think of it—the world is full of music and we might never have developed the ability to make it if we hadn't needed to lull babies to sleep.'

'So,' she said, slanting him a look. His eyes were closed. 'That would make women the original musicians.'

Riley smiled, opened one eye. 'It's only a theory.'

He leaned into the corner of the divan, taking Alexandra and the baby with him. They both froze when Brenna whimpered, shifted and squirmed a bit until she was lying half on Riley, half on Alexandra.

And the entanglement didn't end there. Riley's arm was firmly around Alexandra, his large hand resting familiarly on her ribs. One of her own hands lay on Brenna's back, ready to go into a patting motion at the first squeak out of her, her other hand shifted restlessly around, seeking some neutral ground that didn't involve tousled dark hair, or tanned skin or muscles quite inadequately covered by shirt fabric.

'This is ridiculous,' hissed Alexandra. 'Two adults trapped by one tiny baby. I'm getting up.'

But she no sooner stood up than Brenna let out the ominous cry that they both now recognized as the herald of some serious bawling, and Riley snaked out an arm and dragged Alexandra back while he patted Brenna like mad with his other hand.

'There, there, sweetheart… Don't you dare start her off again! I can't stand the decibels… There, there…' said Riley, all in the same tone. He swung his legs up onto the divan and tucked Alexandra in alongside him, an arm close about her. There was some shuffling and undue rippling of thigh muscles against hers and two muffled thuds sounded as his shoes dropped on the floor. He was barefoot again and she was practically in bed with him.

Alexandra lay very still, closed her eyes and thought unkind thoughts about people who left babies under other people's front stairs.

When she opened her eyes again, the CD had finished and the rain had stopped and there was that interior silence that was never absolute in a house with a tin roof. From outside came the pit-pat of raindrops falling from foliage and the regular 'bo-onk' of the frog that had taken up residence in a neighbour's lily pond.

Slowly, Alexandra turned her head. The man beside her was asleep, dark hair scruffed up, the authoritarian line of his jaw relaxed, his rather nice mouth slightly parted. And held close against his chest was Brenna, her tiny body gently moving to the rhythm of his breathing.

Alexandra held her breath. It was as if she had moved on in time to that point in the future she had always envisioned, when she would not wake up alone but with someone special. That future time when she would have a family of her own.

And here, with this instant family, she tested the feeling she'd always wondered about. How would she feel if this was *her* man, and Brenna their baby? In slow motion, she raised her head and looked at the man. Weak, that's how she felt. At the baby. Strong, weak, worried. At the man. Desire.

She moved with rather more speed and extracted herself from the instant family.

Riley's shoes were in the 'at ease' position on a rug. His mobile phone winked a green light on the far end of the couch. His suit jacket hung on the back of a stool at the breakfast bar, his waistcoat from the corner of the coffee table. His tie lay on the beanbag in the shape of a question mark.

The man was always putting on clothes or taking them off, she thought again. He had not refastened his top shirt buttons and the baby's tiny, smooth fist lay on his hairy chest. Alexandra couldn't drag her eyes away. Something about the contrast between the latent power of the man and the soft helplessness of the child moved her. Riley, as unaware and vulnerable in sleep as the child, had his hands curved around the infant. The red and yellow rattle in its package had fallen to the floor.

Alexandra picked it up. *I will never father children.* How must it feel to know that you would never hold your own child as Riley was now holding Brenna? *Does that seem so terrible to you?* She felt the pain of loss even to imagine it for herself. To her astonishment she felt moisture in her eyes. Not for her own unlikely, imaginable barrenness, but for Riley's.

Awake, he might declare his sterility a good thing in an overpopulated, imperfect world. Asleep, a deep fund of protectiveness and tenderness was revealed in his and Brenna's body language. He cared and the baby knew it and felt safe. No wonder she'd thought for a moment she was in a time warp. Like this, Riley could almost be the man she'd imagined for herself. But of course, he wasn't. This was chemistry, not the stuff on which real love and real life was based. Besides, the man she'd imagined for herself had to be willing to be a father to her children. Willing—and able. Even to think it seemed too cruel.

The rattle made small, tentative sounds as she put it down. She picked up Riley's black shoes, gathered all the items of clothes and folded them together as if she could compress Riley himself into a neat, small, disposable package. She dragged her gaze from the man and child and went to the kitchen to cook her sauce and some pasta. After a moment, she shook out a second serving of pasta into boiling water. Quickly she sliced a couple of her mother's mangoes. The least she could do, she supposed, after all his help, was offer the man a meal.

When the bread was crisping in the oven, her last bottle of wine set on the table with placemats, napkins and glasses, she went gingerly over to remove Brenna to the cot.

'Come on, sweetie,' Alexandra whispered.

Riley groaned. Brenna clung to him, her tiny fist inserted between two shirt buttons and clamped onto his chest hair.

'Oh, come on, love, let go—' Alexandra muttered as she unfastened another of Riley's buttons and tried to prise the baby's hand free. Riley let out another moan and his hand came up to the point of discomfort and clamped over Alexandra's. He opened his eyes to find Alexandra bent low over him. He cast a look down at his gaping shirtfront, at her hand still resting on his bare chest. He let his head drop back and observed her through sleepy, sooty-lashed, half-lidded eyes.

Rain on the roof and the creaks of cooling timber and

iron and the frog calling from the lily pond across the road.

'Did I miss something?'

'No,' she said lightly, doing the best she could as a woman with one hand inside the shirt of a virtual stranger. 'You woke up too soon.'

Riley's smile was catlike. Panther rather than tabby.

'Pretend I'm still asleep.'

'The mood's passed,' she informed him apologetically. 'Besides, I never seduce a man when I'm holding a baby.'

Brenna, who had been twitching, now woke fully and gave a half-hearted cry. Good girl, thought Alexandra, who was inwardly wincing that she had used the word 'seduce.' It hung in the air between them, suggestive of numerous possibilities. See what happens when you just speak without rehearsing first?

Hastily she stood. Brenna's clenched hand took with it several chest hairs and Riley came up off the chair with a strangled howl. She looked back as she went towards the bedroom. Riley rubbed the palm of his hand in a circular motion over his chest. His extraordinary eyes were crinkled in pain and his mouth was as near pouting as a mouth like Riley's would ever get. Barefoot, hair standing on end, a faint shadow on his jaw, his shirt unfastened halfway to the waist, he was a rumpled mess. Alexandra felt the pull of magnetism even from here.

It was now even more important to avoid any further involvement with Riley. She should get him out of here this instant. Tell him to go. Say, 'Thank you so much, Riley, and goodnight. Goodbye.'

'Thank you so much, Riley. Would you like something to eat before you go?'

* * *

Riley found he would. There was a savoury smell coming from the kitchen and a faint, complementary fragrance on his clothes. Herbs, again? He sniffed at his chest. There was something else, something subtle like perfume. But Alexandra didn't wear perfume. From the bedroom came the sounds of Brenna's occasional squawks and Alexandra's voice, softly singing a lullaby by Brahms. In tune, too.

The book on baby care was gone from the carved bookstand which was now back on the dining table bearing the book on herbs.

It was a very old book with pen-and-ink scratched notes in the margins. He turned a page. A line drawing layout of an ideal herb garden. Turned some more. Basil. Thyme. Alexandra had quoted almost word for word from this book. She did not have to rehearse if she knew her material by heart. He grinned.

'Is this valuable?' he asked, looking around as she returned. The static electricity in the air moulded her long wraparound skirt to her thighs. Her hair was loose and curly and shifting *en masse* as she walked. It crackled with static as she stopped beside him.

'Not in monetary terms. It's just a favourite of mine at present. When it came into the shop, I couldn't resist it. I'm building that herb garden in my backyard.' Enthusiasm bubbled in her voice. With an index finger, she sketched out the few alterations she would have to make to the brick paths in the diagram. 'Because I'm recycling the bricks from the cactus planter boxes, and there aren't enough,' she explained.

'Cactus?'

'Oh, I was really into cactus for a while.' She waved a hand to dismiss cactus and pointed to the diagram. Alexandra was very big on diagrams, he thought. 'I'm looking for a sundial to go in the centre, the way it is here. An old one, I hope. With a bit of luck one that I can afford will come up at an auction.'

She cocked an ear at the bubbling sound in the kitchen. 'Sit down, it'll be ready soon.'

Riley sat and turned the pages of *The Herb Lover's Garden*. Sounds of chopping came from the kitchen and a heightening of the scent on his shirt. What the hell had she been handling before she'd been handling him? Once again, he knew it but couldn't bring it to mind. Riley was used to asking questions, not hunting about fruitlessly for answers. He looked at the bottle of wine, turned it to read the label and found a small white sticker that read 'Elderberry.'

'That's the last of my home-made wine,' she told him as she put down a basket of warm bread and a pottery dish of butter. 'I'm afraid I haven't any regular wine to offer you instead.'

'You make your own wine?' he said dubiously, as he poured some of the red liquid into each glass. Damn, and he could use a decent red tonight. The stuff was a good colour at any rate. Here's hoping it was better than her coffee.

'Used to,' she said. 'I came across a book on wine-making in an auction book lot once and just couldn't resist trying it. I used to know the location of every elderberry stand in a five-mile radius, was really keen for a year or so, then—' She shrugged, and one gold-dusted shoulder appeared. Another shrug and it vanished.

Riley swirled a mouthful of wine critically. 'Not bad.'

She grimaced. 'High praise coming from someone who spent his youth in close quarters with fifteen dozen bottles of wine.'

Alexandra went back to the kitchen. Taking his wine-glass, he wandered about the room, crouched at the fire-place to look at the books stacked there. There was

Winemaking for Beginners next to *The Enchantment of Cactus*. Maybe this was where Alexandra stored yesterday's books. One step away from kindling?

He stood and moved away, reading Alexandra's living room for clues to something he couldn't quite articulate.

Alexandra returned bearing a pottery dish in oven-mittened hands. The tip of her tongue showed on her bottom lip as she lowered the steaming, fragrant food to the table. That damned top she wore slipped all over the place again. Light from the kitchen streamed in behind her, flamed the outer wisps of her hair and made her skirt momentarily transparent. He tossed back the elderberry wine and poured more in his glass.

'So,' Alexandra said to break a long silence, but also because she was dying to know. 'Why is your place in such a mess that Caroline invited you to share her bedroom?'

He froze in the act of scraping the last morsel from his plate. 'She didn't say that.'

Alexandra grinned. 'Not in so many words.'

Riley seized the serving bowl to scoop the remainder of the pasta onto his plate. He buttered more bread and bit hugely into it. As he chewed, he looked down his nose at her in that lofty way that probably worked as a deterrent most of the time. At least, on everyone but his mother. As if he realized it would not work on this occasion, Riley sighed.

'Caroline's the daughter of an old friend of the family and just recently she—ah—seems to have—'

'Developed a crush on you? Poor Riley. Women pestering you wherever you go.'

He pulled a face and his hand went to his neck as if he expected to find a tight collar there still. 'She's just eighteen. Basically a nice kid, but she was a late-life child and spoiled. She's sexually precocious and dynamite. I'm trying to back off without hurting any feelings.'

'So—the reason you kissed me was to discourage Caroline.'

'More or less. It seems to be working. She hasn't phoned me once today.' Riley licked a crumb from his lower lip, looked at her mouth. 'What was your reason for kissing me?'

She flushed. Reason had nothing to do with it, which was of course the whole problem. She ignored the faint smile that tweaked the corners of his mouth.

'If you're so keen to discourage Caroline, maybe you shouldn't let her borrow your car,' she said dryly.

'The Judge, her father, borrowed my car. The arrangement was that *he* would pick me up but he let Caroline do it instead.' Riley grimaced again. 'The trouble is, her parents don't exactly discourage her. They—ah—'

'Wouldn't be sorry to see their little bundle of dynamite settle down with a wealthy, father figure from the right kind of family,' finished Alexandra.

Riley's mouth fell open. '"Father figure"?'

She laughed, shrugged. 'Maybe you should consider the idea. She's young and mad about you. Can she cook? The way you've been eating tonight I'm wondering when was the last time you had a square meal. And you're past the marrying age.'

'Caroline's just going through a phase and I've already been married to a girl much like her who was going through a phase, too. It lasted two years and the phase was me. Davina and I were divorced a long time ago.'

'Davina? Your mother mentioned her this morning.'

'My mother,' Riley said heavily, 'entertains hopes of a rematch. Davina left me to marry someone else. She's now divorced again, with two kids this time.' Pause. 'Two little boys who look a bit lost.' He stared into some private distance as he mopped breadcrumbs from his mouth with a napkin. 'If circumstances had been different, they could have been mine.'

Circumstances. Had Davina wanted children? Was that what had made her leave Riley for someone else? And now she was free again and fulfilled as a mother and with Mrs. Templeton championing a rematch. Judging by Riley's pensive expression, he could be considering it. Perhaps he'd never fallen out of love with his ex-wife who had gone off to get what she wanted. Alexandra felt a strong antipathy for the unknown Davina who appeared to have treated him shabbily and was now shaping up for a second term.

She gave herself a mental shake, dismayed to discover herself not only jumping to conclusions, but experiencing a fierce partisanship for this man she'd only met yesterday.

A silence fell. Across the road, the little frog in the pond croaked away, advertising for a mate. Riley buttered the last chunk of crusty bread, mopped his plate with it.

'My place is in a mess,' Riley said, referring back to her question as if nothing had intervened. 'Because it was broken into. Whoever did it threw paint over the walls and floors, used a hammer on the timberwork and doors, wrecked furniture, smashed the kitchen cooktop and the refrigerator. I've been living on microwaved takeaways for the past week.' He licked an index finger and pressed up some residue breadcrumbs from his otherwise empty plate.

'Good grief, Riley—that's shocking.'

'Oh, I don't know. Some takeaway food isn't bad,' he said straight-faced.

She laughed. 'I mean—if you'd been there when they broke in—you might have been hurt.' His eyes flickered and she said without thinking, 'Is this anything to do with those people who were shouting at you?'

Riley considered her thoughtfully. 'Not those particular people. Possibly some others who have—or think they have—a similar grudge against me. It could be a random vandalization. My apartment is in an old building without much in the way of security.'

She rose to collect the plates. Riley followed her into the kitchen and out again, carrying dessert plates while she took the bowl of sliced fruit from the fridge to the table.

She remembered the way he had checked out the street in front of the jazz club. 'Was that why your mother was so suspicious when I tried to get into your office?'

He sighed. 'It was bad luck this all happened while my mother's working in the office. I couldn't keep it from her and now I can't make a move without her watching over me, phoning me at all hours to check that I'm okay. I know she's worried sick, but between her and Caroline…that's why I don't want them to know I go to the club. I need a refuge—' He bent over the fruit, inhaled, clicked his fingers. '*Mango*. Of course!'

Which to Alexandra seemed a very odd response to dessert. Their conversation meandered over family matters. His father, a barrister like *his* father before him, had died in a charter plane accident. Riley had a sister who lived in Zimbabwe with her South African husband and two children. Alexandra told him about her sculptor father, pointed out the sculptures he had willed to her. They argued over art and law and books.

It was almost as if they had met in some nice, normal way and were here together because they wanted to be instead of because they'd been forced into it. As if they were finding each other quite likeable. It wasn't at all tumultuous, or accusing, or critical. It was peaceful.

Brenna woke up and reminded them that they were only here together because of her. The atmosphere became fraught. Alexandra said she hoped that the baby wouldn't wake up crying as often as she had the night before and Riley said, 'Well then, you shouldn't be such a do-gooder.' But they both went to the baby, took turns at holding her, burping her, singing to her.

Brenna was inconsolable when, frazzled, Alexandra lay her in the cot and crouched alongside to sing and stroke her warm little head through the slats. She remained inconsolable until Riley, too, crouched down and added his soothing hand and his voice.

Twenty minutes later, under the joint ministration, she went to sleep.

Twenty-five minutes later, Riley and Alexandra tiptoed out of the room.

In the corridor, they drooped, leaning as one against a crammed bookshelf. Up in the roof a rafter creaked once, then nothing, just the frog across the road. For long, tense moments they waited but Brenna slept and the silence held.

Alexandra and Riley smiled at each other. He raised his right hand, palm outward, and she slapped hers against his in a small victory gesture. It was supposed to be a glancing touch but somehow her hand remained, flat against his.

The air was charged with flying signals. Alexandra felt a shiver down her spine. Goose bumps rose on the warm skin of her forearms. She was experiencing The Chill and without any musical manipulation, just Riley standing close, his shirt hanging open and his hand matched, finger to finger, to hers.

'That frog has been calling like that since November,' she said. 'It lives in a neighbour's lily pond.'

Riley lifted his head and nodded when he tuned in to the rhythmic croak of the frog.

'Why does it do that?' Riley asked. His fingers slid into the spaces between hers, his thumb stroked lengthwise along hers. If this was the equivalent of a change of key, it worked. The Chill zinged down her spine, channelled out in all directions.

'Signalling for a mate, I suppose.'

'Since November? Got to admire his persistence.'

'Or hers. It's a Scarlet-Sided Pobblebonk—according to my frog book.'

'A what? You had a frog period? Was it before, after or between wine-making and cactus? Has the frog book been consigned to the fireplace, too?'

The words went back and forth, ridiculous words that waited out the moment. It was as if they were on the brink of something, not prepared to step back but undecided about going forward. They hardly knew each other, after all. They had nothing in common but a mild curiosity about each other. And chemistry.

Rain started again, lightly tapping on the iron roof.

'I should go,' said Riley. But his palm was warm on hers, his fingers laced with her fingers.

'Yes,' she said, not pretending to misunderstand his meaning.

'You're—er—interested in someone and I don't want to get involved.'

She nodded. 'Same here,' she said, vaguely wondering who it was she was interested in. For the moment she couldn't recall the very sound reasons she had for resisting involvement with Riley, only that she had them. 'So it would be madness to complicate things.'

'Exactly.'

Their hands loosened, drew apart in a slow, relinquishing slide of fingertips until they were two quite separate people again. Riley straightened briskly, looked down and saw his flapping shirt, began working on the buttons. He strode into the living room and sat down to put on his shoes. She collected his tie and jacket and held them out to him. Riley's nostrils twitched, scenting the air. Abruptly he stood and grasped the jacket and tie.

'What *is* that smell?' he muttered, catching her hand to his face. 'Not basil this time, not mango—what is it?'

'Oregano,' she said. 'I picked some from the garden, chopped it for the—' She looked into his eyes. Blue, so blue but warm and smoky and heavy-lidded. '—the— um—the sauce,' she finished breathlessly in a triumph of memory over sensation.

Riley's loose hold on her wrists firmed. She was already moving forward when he hauled her in and she was in his arms.

Any notion that his kiss last night had been a fluke, that her reactions had been the result of the music and anxiety and the headiness of her smoke allergy, was shattered the moment her lips met his. And this time Riley was not staging a kiss for Caroline's benefit. This was no controlled, academic venture but an expression of raw desire.

He crushed her to him, drove a hand into her hair to control the exact tilt of her head and kissed her with a strange kind of finality, as if he had to do it this once but resented it, so must do it quickly.

But Alexandra didn't much care. Just once—what could it matter? She wrapped her arms around him and pressed close, opened her mouth to his and her willingness brought a muffled sound from the back of Riley's throat and every breath, every move, multiplied the intensity until he flexed his fingers on her hips and tipped her body against him so that she felt the imprint of him and the surge of his arousal and the answering pang that was almost pain from deep within her.

On another brink, they paused. Riley gave a smile full of smoke and promises and eased away, let the tumult ebb into delicious anticipation.

His kiss drifted sideways to the tender shadows beneath her jaw, down the column of her neck into the hollow at the base, then to the outer curve of her shoulder exposed by her slip-away top. 'Ummmm,' he sounded, and she felt the swirl of his tongue on her warm skin.

Her senses spun with the pleasure of his touch, with the warmth and the smell of him and the feel of his big, solid body beneath her hands. With shaking fingers she unfastened the buttons of the shirt that he had done up, laughing softly when she found that he had missed a buttonhole, preening at this sign that the learned Riley Templeton had been rattled and because of her.

Her hands slid over his bare chest and suddenly she wasn't laughing at all because Riley's chest was no laughing matter, nor was his broad, silky-smooth back, nor the tight curves of his backside and this quite magnificent curve around here...

Riley groaned.

And it was no laughing matter when he sat on the divan and pulled her down with him so that she sprawled across his knees, one leg exposed by the wraparound skirt to Riley's caressing hand.

Higher he stroked, and higher, and Alexandra uttered little cries of pleasure and felt a strange, insistent rhythm starting up that vibrated through her whole body from its starting point on her calf...

Her *calf?*

Riley stilled at the same moment she did. The insistent rhythm separated itself from the patterns of their breathing. It was the shrill and regular sound of a mobile phone. And she was lying on it. She moved her leg and the sound swelled.

Riley cursed under his breath and fumbled for the mobile. His midnight-blue eyes were fixed on Alexandra. He smoothed one large hand over her thigh, smiling wolfishly at her quick intake of breath as he brushed the backs of his fingers over her underwear.

'Yes?' he said, and for a moment Alexandra thought he was asking consent to proceed. She tumbled the hair from her eyes and almost said 'yes' in reply, but he was talking into the phone.

He sighed, briefly closed his eyes. 'Mum,' he said. 'I'm fine.' He ran a hand through his hair, pulled the edges of his shirt together as if making himself decent for a phone call with his mother. Alexandra would have found it amusing, even endearing, if she hadn't been counting the several ways she had just broken all her own rules.

'Just relax. I'm with a—a friend.' His mouth twitched and he looked up as Alexandra stood, held out a hand to her. 'Mum, stop worrying. I'm okay.' His hand dropped as he watched Alexandra walk away, rewrap her skirt, drag up the neckline of the top so that it covered both shoulders. She came back but only to pick up the jacket and tie that he had flung aside and shake the creases from them. Holding them, she stood waiting, the picture of someone about to see a guest to the door.

'Safer than I could wish, as it happens,' he said sardonically and disconnected.

Riley buttoned his shirt, came over and took the tie from her, looped it about his neck, leaving the ends hanging. He took the jacket from her and shoved the phone back into the pocket. 'Next time,' he said in a low voice, 'I'll switch the damn thing off, drop it in your neighbour's lily pond.'

Alexandra shook her head. 'Look, Riley—I don't think we should—we're just not—suited.'

His eyes narrowed. 'How suited do we need to be? I didn't notice any glaring incompatibility between us just now, did you?'

Alexandra flushed. 'Oh, yes, but you're talking about sex.'

'Darned right.' There was that smokiness still in his eyes and a purposeful glitter.

'That's not everything,' she said lamely.

Riley grinned. 'It's not nothing, either.'

'You don't want to get involved,' she reminded him, feeling harried.

'Maybe I'm—prepared to see where this might lead,' he said.

It was, she decided, the kind of thing the most elusive man said when he wanted an affair. Women needed to think that sex could lead somewhere and men made sure they said the words that women wanted to hear.

'But that's just it,' she said briskly. 'It can't go anywhere because—' Because it was all too impulsive and rash and besides, she knew what she wanted so it was stupid to risk getting involved with someone who didn't—couldn't—be in the picture she had formed of her future. 'Because of—'

'This Gerard character you've been seeing?'

She stared blankly until she remembered the man she was supposed to be involved with. 'Graham,' she corrected, pleased at the solid, intrusive sound of the name.

Riley nodded and looked thoughtful. He walked to the door and she followed, eager for him to be gone, yet dreading it. She had not, she realized, said categorically what she should have said. That there would be no next time. *Finito*. The words just would not come and she hated herself for it. Only the worst, weakest kind of woman teased herself and a man by leaving the door ajar when she should slam it shut. And she intended to eventually slam it shut.

Eventually? Even now, in the secrecy of her thoughts she was equivocating. Was she so weak that she couldn't pass up the opportunity for a few cheap thrills first? Self-disgust kept her silent.

'What I'm going to say now is for your own good, Alexandra.' Perhaps her introspection had made her appear vague, for Riley's voice had taken on the tone of the-man-in-charge.

'I can see that you won't set a deadline for dealing with the baby, so I will. Seven o'clock tomorrow night. If a parent hasn't shown up by then and you don't turn her in, then I will notify the authorities.'

'Turn her in?' she snorted. *For your own good?* Who the devil did he think he was? 'You make her sound like public enemy number one.'

'Seven o'clock.'

'You're being very high-handed, Riley. What gives you the right to 'set limits'?'

He smiled, lightly brushed the backs of his fingers along her jawline.

'My name is on the note, too, remember.'

She was speechless that he would use that, finally, when it suited him. The man was unbelievable. His smile broadened confidently.

'And I know you. You're too soft-hearted to hand over that child and let the mother face the consequences, so I'll take the decision for you and your conscience will be clear.'

Alexandra opened her mouth to utter words of indignation and independence but Riley chose that moment to slide his hands around her waist, stoop to nuzzle in beneath her ear. His lips were warm and moist on her skin and his voice muffled. 'I'd like to stay, but I know, too, that you're not the kind of woman who fools around with two men.' He set her a fraction away from him and smiled, generating a heatwave to compete with the tropical summer. It wrapped around her, prickled at her skin, shortened her breath. 'I'll wait until you give him the bad news.'

'What? Who?' Alexandra said, certain she had misheard him, deafened as she was by the thunder of her pulses.

'Gerard—or Greg or whatever his name is.' Riley's tone was complacent, as if he knew Graham was already ancient history. He bent and kissed her open mouth. 'Make it soon, Alexandra Page.'

And he was gone.

He was the most arrogant, self-important, overopinionated, oversexed man she'd ever met. Alexandra raged into the kitchen where she energetically tossed scraps in the bin for the chickens. One kiss and he was delivering ultimatums and assuming he could read her like a book! The man was so sure of himself that, not only did he think her only reason for not sleeping with him tonight was her conscience over Graham, but that she would cheerfully give the other man the big heave-ho after a few minutes in Riley Templeton's manly arms.

'Think again, Mr. Templeton,' she muttered, slamming down a bowl on the counter. Did he think she would just ditch Graham like that?

Of course, she wasn't attached to Graham at all, but that was beside the point. Riley thought she was.

Her face flamed. How could she have sprawled across his knees like a gift already partly unwrapped for his enjoyment? How could she have practically undressed the man for her own?

Alexandra was vastly relieved to have her original decision justified by Riley's arrogance and overweening complacency. It made it much easier.

She went to the divan and beat all visible traces of

recent activity from the cushions. There was, she reflected, much to be said for nosy, interfering mothers. And for noisy, intrusive technology. What a truly marvellous invention the mobile phone was.

CHAPTER SIX

As IT happened, it was not child welfare officers who called at seven o'clock the next evening, but police officers at six. Through the screen door Alexandra saw the police car turn into her driveway and was transfixed. She looked at Brenna, on a rug on the floor, earnestly shaking the red and yellow rattle, extracted at last from its packaging.

'You louse, Riley.' She ran to the phone, impelled by the sting of betrayal. Riley answered it himself.

'I just wanted to tell you what a louse you are, Riley,' she hissed. 'You said seven o'clock and I thought you were at least a man of your word and I'd have had one more hour to—to get used to the idea.' She heard the sound of an official tread on her front steps, heard Riley say her name but ploughed right on. 'You can relax again, Riley. No more inconvenience, no more embarrassment or twinges of guilt because some poor, lost, desperate mother wrote *your* name with mine. You just can't wait to tear up that note, can you? But then, I suppose you've probably already done that! Well, I hope you sleep well at night.'

She paused to draw in a ragged breath. There was a loud knocking at her front door.

'Alexandra—you're raving. Calm down and reduce this diatribe to either a rational statement or a reasonable question, or I'll hang up.'

'You said *seven o'clock!*' she yelled and banged down the receiver. She picked up Brenna, then went to the door, silently rehearsing. 'Good afternoon, officers. I

know why you're here, of course. Is there a welfare officer with you?'

She wasn't prepared for the steely suspicion of the
officer, nor for the way he stared at the baby then said
over his shoulder to the following policewoman, 'The
child's here and appears unharmed.'

Unharmed?

A half hour later, Alexandra was in a police station, or
in the middle of a nightmare. But you could wake up
from a nightmare, she thought, so it must be a police
station. Alexandra hadn't been allowed to hold Brenna
on the journey in the police car in spite of the fact that
the baby screamed in the arms of the policewoman.
Alexandra had been marched inside under close super-
vision whereupon a swollen-eyed, weeping young
woman had given out a strangled cry at the sight of
Brenna and held out her arms to take the baby. A young
man with long hair put his arm around her and leaned
over the child.

Alexandra wiped a few tears from her own eyes at the
reunion. She moved forward to say how glad she was
about it, but the WPC and the young man barred her
way.

'Is she the one who stole my daughter?' the angry
young man demanded of no one in particular.

An angry older woman then stepped forward. 'Is this
the woman who kidnapped Savannah?' she demanded of
the young mother.

'Savannah?' Alexandra said. 'So that's her na— *kidnapped?* What do you mean, kidnapped?'

'What kind of a woman are you?' snarled the young
man. 'Stealing other people's kids from supermarkets—
you ought to be locked up!'

'If Pam was looking after her properly, no one would
get close enough to snatch her, Jeffie,' the older woman

complained. 'It's not right—some people would do *any-thing* to have a little girl like that. Some people would go through years of tests and disappointments and still not have one—and a silly little tart like you just has one by accident!' The woman glared at the weeping young mother.

Jeffie shook his head. 'I've told you, Mum. Don't call Pam a tart.'

The young mother hugged her baby and looked at Alexandra with a crushed, apologetic air rather than condemnation, as well she might.

'Look, I never said anything about *snatching*—' she began, but her voice went unheard by the vocal young man and his shrill mother. There was a bout of official peacekeeping in the form of 'Now then, Mrs. Brown, Anna—' and 'Let's take it easy, shall we, Mr. Brown, Jeff—'

But young Mr. Brown wasn't done. He was in fine temper and loud about it. 'I'm away a few days fishing with some mates and I get a call from my mother—to come home straight away because she's called to see Pam and the baby isn't there and Pam won't say where she is! It's only when I get home at last that Pam tells me *you've* got our daughter and gone off with her and she's been in a state about it all afternoon and too damned stupid to call the police.'

'Jeff, I never said—' said Pam, ineffectually.

'Everyone feels sorry for women like you, but I don't. If you can't have kids of your own, that's no excuse to go kidnapping other people's. I'm going to press charges.'

Alexandra glanced at Pam, who wouldn't meet her eyes, then took a firm stance for self-preservation. 'Look—you've got it all wrong—let me tell you exactly how I came to be in charge of your baby.' But at that point, she intercepted a look of such pain and pleading from Pam that she fell silent. The young woman looked at Jeff then back at Alexandra and gave the small shake of the head that was understood by women the world over. 'He doesn't know.'

Alexandra wondered why she was passing this message so secretively when it was obvious that Jeff didn't know she'd left the baby bundled up on a stranger's doorstep. Unless Pam was trying to tell her something else.

Alexandra studied the muscular, angry young father who was intimidating merely on the basis of volume. She studied his mother whose eyes dwelt hungrily on her grandchild. The woman's voice seemed only a shade away from hysteria. 'The poor little scrap is sickly because you wouldn't even try to breastfeed her and she hasn't even been christened yet, though it seems a sin to christen any child 'Savannah'! I can't imagine where you got such a ridiculous name.'

Alexandra quailed. There were too many explosive emotions at work in this family. She imagined Pam, distraught at her own actions, unable to admit she'd left their baby on someone's doorstep, forced to fabricate something to explain the child's absence for two days to the child's fond—no, obsessive—grandmother who was eager to label her irresponsible.

Her eyes widened. What had Jeff said? That Pam was beside herself 'all afternoon'? If all his explosive anger and contempt was because he thought the baby had gone missing just today, heaven help Pam if he found out the full extent of it.

If it came out here, Pam would be liable to official action and the young father might eventually forgive her for that but not for making a prize fool of him so publicly. But that's not my problem, thought Alexandra. The girl *had* dumped her baby and it was hard to imagine even a scolding, neurotic mama-in-law was sufficient reason for that. Maybe she would be better off in the hands of officialdom. Maybe she needed psychiatric assessment and help.

Impatiently Alexandra tried to reject her own resistance to commonsense. After all, if she'd phoned the police the moment she found the child, none of this would be happening. If Pam could abandon her baby, then surely she, Alexandra, had a perfect right to abandon Pam. Or so she thought, even as she knew she would override commonsense.

'Look—' she began, rehearsing and rejecting various ways of removing babies from supermarkets without incriminating herself or blowing the whistle on Pam. In desperation, she sat down, folded her arms and said, 'It's all a mistake. I'm saying nothing until I've phoned my lawyer.'

A harried police officer said that was not necessary as she was not under arrest at the moment, but she was adamant. There was no privacy for her call, so Alexandra had to keep her explanations basic.

'Ah, Alexandra,' Riley drawled. 'Have you phoned to finish your assassination of my character? I fear I have only five minutes to spare. Will that be time enough, do you think?'

'Riley. I'm at a police station. Brenna's parents and grandmother have shown up—Jeff and Pam and um—his mother, Anna Brown. I—might be charged with kidnapping. I need you, Riley.' She hadn't meant to say that, had only meant the phone call to stall proceedings until she could think of some way out.

There was only the barest pause. 'Jeff and Pam. Which station?' said Riley in clipped neutral tones that instilled her with confidence. 'I'm on my way.'

Sweeter words she'd never heard. It astounded her that she had so much faith in Riley, though what he could do to extricate her from this mess she couldn't imagine.

Time passed. A doctor arrived and the parents and baby went away with her for a time. Alexandra's face flamed as various people looked curiously at her. Did they think she had *harmed* the child?

The family came back at the same time as Riley arrived. In the past she had found his appearances annoying, intimidating, disturbing. For the first time Alexandra found the sight of his tall figure, those cool, composed features unconditionally gladdening. Alexandra sighed and smiled broadly when he looked her way. His response was an ironic little twist of the lips that put a quick end to any feelings of gladness.

He turned to study Pam, who looked blankly back. Jeff bristled. He hefted an accusatory forefinger in Alexandra's direction. 'You might be able to afford a fancy lawyer, lady, but we'll press charges anyway. People like you ought to be behind bars!'

'I think we can clear this up immediately,' Riley said when the duty officer came forward. He reached inside his jacket and produced two tattered pieces of paper.

Pam's face blanched.

Oh, God, Alexandra thought, it was the note!

Just for a moment they all stood there, eyes on Riley's authoritative hand. Then Alexandra hurried forward, plucked the two fragments of the note from him and tore them in halves.

Riley's mouth dropped open. 'What the hell are you doing?'

His hand made a couple of bereaved moves in the direction of the note, his major piece of evidence. Alexandra ripped it into pieces and was about to fling the bits in a nearby waste bin, but a sudden vision of a bored PC or Jeff's mother taping them together again made her stuff them into her pocket.

Alexandra fixed the startled Riley with a meaningful gaze. He had such beautiful, dark blue eyes. She almost forgot what she had to say.

'This has all been a terrible misunderstanding, Mr. Templeton. I shouldn't have called you out, it really isn't necessary. I was just baby-sitting for Pam, you see,' she said, hoping desperately that both he and Pam would follow up with something that could be believed. 'Met her at the supermarket to take Brenna—Savannah.' As she turned to Pam she saw Riley blink and his mouth silently form the name 'Savannah.'

'What on earth made you think I'd kidnapped her, Pam?'

Pam's body had sagged in relief and now tensed again. 'I—it's—' She floundered. 'I never *said* you kidnapped her—I—um—what really happened was—um—'

'Come on, Pam!' Alexandra said bracingly. The girl surely couldn't run out of story-telling ability at this crucial point? She dug in her pocket and opened her hand so that Pam could see the bits of the note, still reclaimable. It was as successful as a cattle prod.

'Um—well—we agreed I'd come to pick her up at your place—and—I came to your place, and—um—'

'And—I wasn't there,' Alexandra finished, picking up her cue. She gave a laugh. 'Well, of course I wasn't there. Don't you remember, I told you—that is, I asked you if I could—take Br—Savannah out.'

'Out where?' demanded Jeff.

'Oh—um—' Alexandra swallowed hard. She was not good at this. She needed time to rehearse quite ordinary things, was no good at thinking on her feet. Her eyes went to Riley.

'To your mother's place,' he said smoothly.

Alexandra blinked at him. Poker-faced, he went on to the company at large. 'Ms. Page's mother is the well-known portrait artist, Rhona Thompson. She needed an infant model for a subject in a forthcoming painting. Your daughter—' he inclined his head at Jeff '—proved to be an excellent model. Ms. Thompson has several excellent working sketches, but of course, should she decide to use them without alteration in a permanent work, she will seek your permission first.'

This was a man who truly could think on his feet. A respectability not normally associated with artists was somehow brought to the situation with the introduction of the well-known Rhona Thompson. Jeff, suddenly finding himself the father of a child likely to be captured in art for posterity, was partially mollified.

'I expect I didn't communicate very well with Pam about that. She might have thought I meant to take Savannah to my mother's studio another day.'

'Yes, I did,' said Pam, her eyes glazed over with this sudden development.

'How could you get something like that wrong?' Mrs. Brown the elder said scornfully, more interested, it seemed, in undermining Pam's reputation as a mother, than in the dubious logic of the claims being made.

'Of course, you do know that Miss Page was only last week awarded a Police Medal for bravery,' said Riley, looking around with a slight frown when it became apparent that this was news to everyone but Pam. 'She rescued three children from a house fire, last year, sustaining considerable burns herself in the process. Your— baby-sitter is a heroine.'

Sam must have blabbed, thought Alexandra. She felt Riley's eyes on her and looked away, hot and uncomfortable with the tag of heroine.

'I *thought* that name sounded familiar,' said the WPC. She grinned. '"Alexandra the Great" they called you in the newspapers.'

Alexandra grimaced.

Jeff, sulky and embarrassed, cast about for some saving grace. 'Well, how come you never mentioned this—Miss Page before and how did you meet her anyway?' he challenged Pam.

The girl looked to Alexandra for deliverance.

'At my bookshop,' Alexandra said, with a sense of *déjà vu.*

Now Jeff really did look suspicious. *'Bookshop?'* he hooted. Clearly Pam was not a keen reader.

'I have a very comprehensive baby-care section,' Alexandra said, telling no lies.

'Oh.' Jeff looked uneasily at his mother, then at Pam. 'You should have *told* me Miss Page was okay,' Jeff said, his face red. 'I would've waited a while longer instead of rushing off to the police.'

'I tried to tell you—everything. But your mother—' She bit her lip. 'Everyone kept shouting and no one ever *listens* to me.'

Jeff looked resentful. 'A famous artist wants to draw our kid and you don't even tell me about it?' he accused, and seemed to find the idea suspicious as soon as he voiced it.

Alexandra closed her eyes briefly. Just how many bridges were there to cross before they could get out of here?

Pam burst into tears. 'I wanted to surprise you,' she said.

CHAPTER SEVEN

IT WAS Riley who got them out of there, with some smooth, fast-talking with a senior officer who was glad to get rid of the crazy bunch once he was certain there was no charge to answer. It was Riley who arranged a taxi for Jeff's mother and saw her quite firmly into it. It was Riley who led the way out, his long-striding figure the focus for the straggle of three plus baby that followed. They carried their emotional baggage with them—Jeff, his embarrassment and resentment, Pam, her guilt, Alexandra, her relief and a contradictory sense of bereavement.

'Thank you so much—' Pam whispered to Alexandra. 'Did she—was she good? I hope she wasn't any trouble...sometimes she grizzles a lot...'

'Trouble? Good heavens—I only had to close the shop early two days in a row and rearrange my whole house and routine! Think nothing of it!' Alexandra said, suddenly intensely annoyed with the girl. Had she been having a nice little holiday while she, Alexandra, was caring for her child? But the girl's bitten fingernails suggested otherwise. 'I gave her goat's milk in her last bottle. She seemed to digest it more easily.'

'Two days?' said Jeff, his resentment dissolving readily into suspicion again. 'I thought you'd only had Savannah with you today.'

Alexandra glanced at Pam. The girl would have to give him the whole story sooner or later. But she merely said, darkly, 'It *seemed* like two days.'

Riley whirled to face them. They were in the car park now with the last of the dusk fading and the humid heat

110

of summer pierced by the stop-and-start-again shrill of cicadas from the drooping paperbark trees. With the accumulated heat of day beating up at them from the concrete, the three adults chilled in the cold blast that emanated from Riley.

'Quiet!' he said, and even the cicadas stopped for the space of three heartbeats. 'We will go to my chambers and sort this out,' he snapped. Jeff opened his mouth and Riley's gaze homed in on this prelude to argument, crushed it. 'Now,' he added. His car lights flashed as he pressed the remote. 'Get in.'

He held open the door for the young couple, standing like some stern sentinel over them. But he reached out and placed a protective hand over the baby's head as Pam carried her into the back seat. Something about the way he did it made tears prick at Alexandra's eyes. His anger was as vibrant in the air as the buzz of cicadas, yet his hand curved with extraordinary gentleness around the tiny, vulnerable skull, adding his care to the mother's.

He closed the door on the family and strode around to open the door for Alexandra. She smiled brilliantly at him, impulsively laid a hand on his arm.

'Thanks for everything, Riley. You were fantastic tonight—you caught on so fast. I couldn't have managed without you. But are you sure it's a good idea to go to your chambers, now? After all, they're in an emotional state and it's time the baby was bathed and—'

Riley removed her hand from him, used the grip to propel her toward the front door. 'Get in,' he said between clenched teeth.

Alexandra blinked. She had expected to find herself acknowledged as his fellow sufferer at the hands of the young parents, instead of which he seemed more furious with her than with them. 'Why are you so upset with *me?*' she demanded in an injured tone. 'What happened tonight isn't *my* fault!'

His teeth, still clenched, were displayed momentarily in a snarl. 'And did you notice what *didn't* happen tonight, Miss Page, tireless righter of wrongs?'

She flushed at the sarcasm. 'What?'

'There was no fond reunion. No friendly "Hi, how are you?" No recognition of one acquaintance for another.' Grimly he watched her review the last hour.

'Oh,' she said, remembering Pam's blank expression and the lack of recognition in his own scrutiny.

'Exactly. The writer of that famous bloody note you've been shoving under my nose with monotonous regularity doesn't know me from Adam.'

Alexandra bit her lip. She'd badgered him, invaded his privacy, waved that note at him to activate his conscience.

'Goodness. It must have been some other Riley,' she said weakly.

She thought she heard a grinding noise. 'And you even had me beginning to think it was fate or something that our names turned up together on that— Get in,' he said.

She got in and trod on a parcel.

Alexandra stooped to pick up a large paper carrier bearing the David Jones department store name. Riley whisked it from her grasp, muttering something, but not before she had a glimpse of the contents.

'A teddy bear?' she said, looking up at him. His eyes slid away from hers. If anything he was even more wrathful now that she'd seen the big honey bear with its tartan bow. The door slammed, he stabbed at his remote and the boot lid opened then closed again as Riley disposed of his shopping.

He didn't look at her at all and didn't speak as the car swung out into traffic towards the city. A dead silence reigned except for Savannah, who gurgled and cooed the whole of the drive to the Inns of Court.

He led the way along the lushly furnished corridors to his chambers, nodding brusquely to a cleaner who looked enquiringly up from vacuuming. Inside, he bypassed the low, comfortable lounge chairs and indicated the more businesslike ones before the desk. He seated himself without ceremony and Alexandra wondered if he knew how formidable he looked, entrenched behind the desk's broad, antique expanse.

'Your baby,' he said to Jeff, 'was left under Miss Page's front steps two nights ago.'

Pam gasped and began to cry. Jeff's mouth dropped open.

'And before you start criticising, you will listen, without interruption, to Pam's reasons for taking this action.'

It took some time. Pam cried so much that she started the baby off and at length agreed to let Alexandra hold Savannah. The story came out in fits and starts. Pam's parents lived in Victoria and couldn't afford to come up to Queensland to visit. Jeff's parents—more particularly his mother—thought she, Pam, was too young and silly to care for a baby and wanted to take Savannah from her and bring her up.

'How old are you, Pam?' said Riley.

'Nearly eighteen.'

The dead silence that greeted this as Riley and Alexandra did their sums spurred Pam to temporary defiance. 'Everyone tells me off for having a baby because I'm too young—I stopped going to the baby clinic because they made me feel stupid and they used to *admire* all the other babies but treated mine like they felt sorry for her!'

Alexandra was relieved to hear some healthy indignation from the passive and depressed Pam.

While Jeff was away, Anna Brown told Pam she had

been to the child welfare and reported her as an unfit
mother, that the baby would be taken from her in the
next few days if she didn't see sense and hand Savannah
over to her grandparents. Pam had come in from emp-
tying the waste once to find Anna Brown taking the baby
from her cradle. She'd had to fight to get the child off
the older woman.

'You'd given her a key,' she said to Jeff. 'And I'd
asked you not to.'

'She was probably just giving her a cuddle,' Jeff said,
but it was a weak protest.

'She had a carry-cot with her, the kind you strap onto
a car seat. I didn't know what to do. She had a *key*. You
weren't here. I felt like I was going out of my mind,
worrying about it,' Pam said to Jeff, smearing black
mascara over her nose with the back of her hand. 'If
your mother took her, the welfare people might think I
didn't want her and you'd side with your parents and I
might never get her back.'

'I wouldn't!' said Jeff, horrified.

'Why didn't you go to the police?' asked Riley.

'I didn't want to get Jeff's mum into trouble. She—
she just wants a baby girl so badly, she doesn't know
what she's doing.'

Riley phoned for a cab and explained Pam's legal
rights as a mother, provided the name of a counsellor
that Anna Brown might be persuaded to consult. It was
Jeff who took the baby, and Alexandra stifled a protest
as the warm little body slipped through her fingers. Pam
looked back from the door, glowing, said, 'Thanks,' and
suddenly they were gone.

Riley stayed at the door, looking out.

'Oh.' Alexandra blinked on some welling tears.
'That's it, then.'

Riley closed the door, took off his jacket, tossed it
aside and put his hands on his hips.

'Are you mad? Are you some new kind of adrenalin junkie? Why the hell don't you just take up rock-climbing without a rope?'

'What?' Sniffing, Alexandra fished in her bag for a tissue.

He came over and took a strong hold on her upper arms, giving a small shake to force her to look up at him.

'Don't you realize you were in a very serious position? A charge of kidnapping is—very serious.' He gave her another shake as if annoyed to find he was repeating himself. Alexandra sniffed and resumed her search for a tissue. 'You could have been in real trouble,' he yelled.

Alexandra located a tissue, dabbed at her eyes and gave him a brilliant smile. 'I know. That's why I phoned you, Riley. And you were terrific—'

'Terrific?' he bellowed. He strode away from her, tugging at his tie knot, thrusting his head from side to side as he loosened it and unfastened his collar button. 'I was treading dangerously close to contempt, that's what I was doing. And all because *you*—' he spun around in a move that was extraordinarily graceful for such a tall, solid man, and pointed that practised index finger at her.

'You had to play Mary Poppins to protect an over-wrought, middle-aged neurotic and a silly kid who should have been still in school instead of incubating another child. Don't you know *you* could have ended up catching the legal flak? You had to meddle, didn't you, instead of letting them suffer the consequences of their own actions!'

'Yes, I was a bit worried there for a while,' she admitted. 'But I couldn't let poor Pam be exposed as an abandoning mother in that setting. You know yourself, the police would have been obliged to bring in a social worker...and as it turned out Pam was quite valiantly trying to keep Jeff's pathetic mother out of trouble, so I can't help feeling I did the right thing.'

'Poor Pam? Pathetic Mrs. Brown?' he said in exasperation. 'The girl has no business having a baby at her age and in her circumstances, and your pathetic Mrs. Brown is a carping, monstrous woman.'

Alexandra nodded. 'Yes, but only because she wanted a daughter and couldn't have one, I think. It must be terrible to want something so badly—' She fell silent, uneasy with the portrait of Anna Brown, so obsessed with her wish for a girl child that she had become insensitive to anyone or anything else.

Riley paced around, discarded his waistcoat. He was, Alexandra thought, getting perilously short of clothes to take off. A certain melancholy had intruded on her mood, but she felt a powerful warmth towards Riley that his wrath couldn't shift. He rolled up his shirt sleeves and glared, and it should have been an intimidating sight. Alexandra found herself admiring his splendid forearms and the peculiar grace of his large, blunt-fingered hands as they snapped and rolled the sleeve fabric with the same precision that they had performed the delicate task of unfastening tiny cuff buttons.

''I was just baby-sitting for Pam... Don't you remember, I asked you if I could take Savannah out...''' He mimicked and finished with a snort.

'I was absolutely stuck at that point,' Alexandra confessed. 'When Jeff said ''where?'' I couldn't think of a thing. That was a brainwave of yours, Riley. What on earth made you think of my mother and a portrait? It was perfect.'

'Spare me the blandishments,' he said, eyes narrowed. 'The point is, you went out on a limb, lied to the police and destroyed the only evidence of your own innocence.'

'But I knew you'd get me out of it, Riley. I knew

you'd get us all out of it, and you did.' Her faith in him had a negative effect.

His hands descended on her shoulders. With a face as black as thunder he said, sounding out every syllable in a low, furious tone, 'I'm a lawyer. My father was a lawyer and his father and his, not to mention all the men in my mother's family. I have my own reputation and theirs to uphold and I *lied*, I misled the authorities. I allowed that *bloody* note to be ripped up in front of the police while charges of kidnapping were being touted and you were playing irresponsible games.' He dragged her forward and upward so that he looked ferociously into her face.

'You aren't obliged to run into *every* burning building, you know. It's sheer ego to think you've got to be the heroine who saves everyone who ever messed up their lives.'

Alexandra was white-faced. 'That's not fair.'

'If I hadn't taken over tonight, you'd be sitting in a coffee shop somewhere now, commiserating with the poor young people—encouraging them to lean on you, practically *inviting* them to depend on you the next time they suffer some crisis—and it's a funny thing how often crises occur when you have someone waiting in the wings to nobly bear the burden. I'm not sure why you do it—'

'Can I be hearing right?' she bit out. 'Riley Templeton not *sure?*'

'Maybe it's your way of earning distinction because you missed out on the talent in your family, ''Alexandra the Great.'' '

It was a double thrust. She felt the hurt right down to her boots.

'You're right,' she said in a clear, high voice. 'I did miss out on the talent in my family, but if you think I believe that rubbish they wrote about me in the press you're mistaken. They gave a bravery medal to an imposter. I saw the flames that day and nearly didn't stop.'

'Alexandra,' he said with a rueful air, 'I was merely using that as a metaphor, I didn't mean to cast doubt on your rescue of those—'

'I remember being angry because no one else was around and I would have to—do something,' she went on, driven by the shame that had dogged her since that day. 'I didn't want to get involved.'

'Ah, now I'm beginning to see,' said Riley, nodding.

'I—remember shouting "Is anyone inside?"' she said. 'I remember thinking, 'I hope I don't have to go in there because I'm allergic to smoke."'

Riley took in a deep breath. 'So, of course, when a baby was delivered to your front door with a plea from its mother, you *had* to get involved, to atone.'

'If there'd been anyone else around—*anyone*—I wouldn't have done it and I was expecting to be exposed as a fraud all during that medal ceremony. You can call me a coward and you can call me a hypocrite for turning up to be given a medal I didn't deserve, but don't you *dare* call me a heroine!'

Riley gave a huff of laughter, raised his eyes to the ceiling. It was not the reaction she'd expected.

'Afterwards I howled louder than the kids I carried out. I threw up, too, in front of the press,' she went on, taking a savage pleasure in exposing every shameful little detail.

'The press has that effect on a lot of people,' Riley said dryly.

She gave a shaky laugh.

'Anyway, whatever my motivation for acting as I did tonight, no one *forced* you to go along with it. No one *pressured* you to make up stories about baby portraits.'

'You mean I had a choice when you said, "Oh, Riley, I need you"? When you turned those big, imploring, grey eyes on me and practically begged me to come up with something?'

She was taken aback by his vehemence. 'I didn't *implore* you,' she said. But whatever he thought he'd seen in her big grey eyes, he hadn't been able to resist. It was very gratifying. She was aware that it was something she should think about more deeply, but right now it was enough that he had handed her the advantage in an argument. Triumphantly, Alexandra jabbed a forefinger at his shoulder.

'That's why you're so furious. Because you went along with it all, instead of doing things by the book! Well, you can't blame me for that.'

'Can't I?' Riley caught her hand before she could withdraw it. His other arm went around her waist, pulling her close to him in a move that had great authority yet still allowed for objections. She had only to blink and he would release her, she just knew that. Alexandra breathed in the smell of him and gazed into his extraordinary eyes and didn't blink at all.

Riley acknowledged her willingness with a glint in his eyes and some subtle fingering on her back that produced The Chill of a musical change of key. His voice was low, muted, and he looked at her mouth while he spoke.

'No matter how you felt about it, you should have told the police that you were awarded that medal by the commissioner.'

Alexandra watched her fingers slide beneath his unbuttoned shirt collar. Beneath the thin shirt fabric the bone and muscle of his shoulders formed splendid contours. Absently, she shrugged a shoulder. 'It didn't seem relevant.'

Riley made a throaty sound and released her hand to stroke her shoulder. It was bare but for the strap of her black singlet top. Alexandra shivered.

'You didn't think it was relevant to tell me that Dad's portrait had been painted by your mother, either.' He inclined his head toward the portrait.

'What did that have to do with anything?'

Riley let his mouth drift over her shoulder, nudged aside the strap. 'That sort of thing can give you an edge. Name-dropping, wearing your medals—it means you don't have to start from scratch in every situation. It's the way the world works.'

'I'm not sure how you—um—work the details of a medal into a screaming match over a kidnapped baby,' she said breathlessly. 'And would it have made you want to help me sooner if I'd pointed to your father's portrait and said, "My mum painted that"?'

Riley's head dipped lower. 'It—has a certain fatalistic element that you could have used in your favour. Your mother painted my father long before we'd even met. It gives us a connection, a history almost. It might have made it seem less crazy that my name was on a note with yours…as if it was fate or something. Mmmm.'

Her hands slid around the nape of his neck. 'I don't believe you would have fallen for anything so irrational, Riley.'

Riley smiled. 'But you should at least have tried it. Always a good idea to press your advantage,' he said as he peeled the thin, black straps down over her arms and the flimsy top with it.

His big hands framed her bare breasts. Her gasp of pleasure was sharp and shocking in the book-lined room. His thumbs flexed, manipulating a repetition of the sound, circled, for another, stroked across her nipples, each passage drawing the same sighing sound from her. Alexandra felt the edge of Riley's desk behind her and sank backwards, her upper arms tethered by the straps, her breasts exposed to him. 'Always a good idea,' he repeated huskily.

He eased her back and back onto the desk surface, straight-arming a sheaf of papers out of the way. They overshot the far edge and spilled to the floor in a pigeon flutter and she would always afterwards associate the sound with the exact sensation of Riley's mouth at her breasts.

'Oh, Riley—' she breathed. Her fingers curled into his thick, dark hair as she arched back, doubly seduced by the suck of Riley's mouth on one nipple, and the tingling, moist trace of him on the other.

From some other world came the sounds of a television with the volume turned low. One voice answering another. A whining sound. A thump. The volume turned up. And up. Actual words drifted through the cracked door.

'—could leave this suite until last, would you mind? My son's working late and—'

Alexandra froze. Riley shot to his feet, uttering one short, sharp Anglo-Saxon word. He hauled Alexandra up and went to work on his buttons, drove a hand through his hair. 'I have to find her something to *do,*' he muttered under his breath. 'Climbing Everest, circumnavigating the globe, *anything* to take her mind off my life! Forty-five charity committees just doesn't use up enough of her energy!'

Frantically, Alexandra straightened her clothes. By the time Fiona Templeton opened the door, her elegant hands full of food cartons and fruit, Alexandra and Riley were at opposite ends of the desk.

'—knew you'd probably work on without eating and if you go home you'll only heat up something despicable in your microwave,' Mrs. Templeton said before she noticed Alexandra. She stopped. Eyed her son, then Alexandra, and whatever small clues she saw in their appearance put a frost on her beautifully made-up face.

'Dear me,' she said, looking down her nose as if she'd

just discovered her son with the scullery maid. Then, turning her attention exclusively to Riley, said, 'Is this wise, Riley? You know it is not a good idea to allow a woman in your chambers when you have no staff around. You leave yourself open to—' Her eyes flicked over Alexandra. 'All kinds of—allegations.'

Alexandra grabbed her bag. For a moment there, she thought the woman had been about to say 'diseases.'

'I see you haven't brought the baby this time,' Mrs. Templeton said, and it was difficult to say whether she thought this was a good or a bad thing. On the one hand its screams were not Disturbing the Peace. On the other, it might have kept her son and his visitor too busy to venture into the other activities she clearly suspected. Alexandra's face flamed. She felt stupid, adolescent and unequal to dealing with Riley's formidable, snobbish mother.

'Dare I hope you have—em—brought that little matter of the child to resolution, Miss—em—'

'Page,' said Alexandra, grabbing her bag. 'And yes, you may dare hope. I'm just leaving.' The woman oozed superiority. If there was ever an occasion when she could use an advantage, it was now. As she passed her, Alexandra pointed at the portrait. 'By the way, my mother painted that.'

Mrs. Templeton raised one eyebrow, her hostility diminished not one bit by this piece of name-dropping. Alexandra threw a speaking glance at Riley before she fled.

She considered taking a cab home but none cruised past and she walked, in light rain, to her shop and let herself in. Aimlessly, she drifted around the shelves, straightening spines, retrieving the odd fallen book, setting aside several paperbacks with loose pages. She felt the depression that sometimes strikes suddenly, after too

much champagne, when the laughing and the bubbles
stop and the alcohol swamps the liver.

It was a long time since she'd had too much champagne. But too much Riley looked likely to cause an
even bigger hangover. She paused in Natural History,
closed her eyes. Cringed. What was the matter with
them? They couldn't keep their hands off each other.

If Fiona Templeton hadn't breezed in with a gourmet
feast for her only boy, the cleaning staff might have
crept up noiselessly on the lush carpet and found her and
Riley at an even later stage of events. God, how awful.
Even so, she felt a pang deep below her navel as if some
elemental part of her was saying to hell with the potential embarrassment and why did Fiona Templeton have
to butt in?

Confused, she snatched from the shelf a book that
belonged in Biology. Whether she was glad or not that
his mother had shown up when she did was surely academic now, anyway.

Someone knocked on the glass front. She went to the
door, jiggled the Closed sign, then saw that it was
Graham who peered in with both hands cupped around
his temples.

'Just passing—had to work late and delay my run,' he
told her when she opened the door. He wore running
shorts, a singlet and trainers and his tan skin was slick
with perspiration. 'I headed off on Eagle and Wickham
to the Valley, cut through to Boundary and back along
Gregory Terrace, through Albert Park and down George
into Elizabeth—saw your light on.'

'Hello, Graham,' she said, and opened the door wide.
Graham always felt the fullest details of his running
route were necessary but tonight she was almost glad of
it to distract her. 'Want a cup of coffee?'

Graham looked askance and she remembered that, of
course, he didn't drink coffee because the caffeine inter-

fered with his pulse rate while he was in training for his next triathlon. He took a swig from a water bottle at his waist and checked the book she carried.

'Ah.' He took it from her enthusiastically, reclipping the bottle at his waist. 'Now this is a very interesting book on evolutionary theory...'

Graham was off on his second favourite subject. While he talked, Alexandra set to work on a loose page into a paperback and marked the price down, pondering the mysteries of physical attraction. Here was Graham, generally regarded as a hunk by the female staff of the boutique next door, wearing next to nothing and smelling elementally of sweat and good, clean exertion, flashing some fabulous teeth at her and her mind kept wandering.

On his *desk*.

Spread wantonly on its antique surface.

With the portrait of his father, painted by her mother, looking on. It was almost doing it at a family gathering! Shame didn't preclude her reliving certain sensual highlights.

Graham flicked through the book, letting the pages flutter to rest at a diagram.

'—See this—you have to marvel, don't you, at the miraculous design of the human hand with its opposing thumb that makes it capable of the subtlest of tasks—'

She did marvel, her hands fleetingly laid to her breasts. The human thumb, she agreed, was a wonderful thing.

Graham gave her the book, took his pulse and said he had to get moving down Albert towards the Gardens, along Margaret and cut through Felix to his office on Eagle. He said something about tomorrow night and by the time he'd left, she understood she had agreed to meet him for a late-night movie. Almost, she called him back to say she couldn't go out with him after all, but Graham had already covered a great deal of ground and she shrugged and decided it was just as well that she got back to normal.

Brenna was back with her parents. Everything had turned out just fine. It hadn't been Riley's name on the note. She and Riley had only been in this thing together by mistake. The thing to do now was to finish it, put it all behind her, and soon it would be as if none of it had ever happened.

She wondered about that. She'd seen her mother paint a coat of ultramarine over a thin wash of white that had accidentally picked up the tiniest bit of red.

Once it is there, no matter how much you paint on top of it, it remains, Rhona had told her. That tiny bit of red couldn't be neutralised. It influenced the colours painted over it and made the whole painting turn out differently.

Alexandra took a bus home. The first skirmishes of a storm rattled banana palms and set bougainvillaea boughs swaying on the fences as she walked home from the stop. She thought of Brenna, the baby she'd looked after for only a day or two, and felt bereft. She thought of Brenna's grandmother, her face turned ugly by obsession for a girl child she could never have. She thought of Riley and uncontrollable impulses that could suddenly divert a person's life onto a path she never wanted to tread. An exotic, jungle path that promised adventure and gratification but would probably end up on the edge of the cliff of unfulfillment.

Before she went inside, she fished the torn pieces of the note from her pocket and let them go. The first wind gusts of the storm swirled them high into the air.

CHAPTER EIGHT

GRAHAM had a way of explaining away perfectly pleasant things in technical ways. Once, in Moreton Bay, when she commented on the magical sheen on the water, Graham said, 'What's really happening here, Alexandra, is that the light reflected from the water is entering the pupils of your eyes at the rate of 10 trillion particles of light per second, setting off a biochemical sequence that—' Blah, blah—

During the two days that followed the reunion of baby Brenna with her parents, Alexandra discovered a new sensitivity to the sound of the telephone. Each time it rang, she experienced a quickening of pulses, a faint tremor of the hands and a dryness in her throat. No doubt Graham would put it down to differences in oxygen intake due to a crisis response originating in the adrenal glands, or some such thing.

What no one, including Graham, could explain was why Riley Templeton—a man she'd known for a matter of days—should be having any effect on her glands, adrenal or otherwise. For it was his voice she half expected to hear every time she answered the phone.

She had, of course, rehearsed what she would say. 'Riley, I don't think it's a good idea to go on seeing each other.' Or, 'Riley—let's call it a day. It wasn't your name on the note and I should never have bothered you about the baby. We shouldn't even have met.'

Yes, she had it all under control. She knew what she wanted in life…a man who valued her for a whole range of qualities quite separate from sex appeal. And children. She wanted her own children. It was tempting to consider an affair with Riley but she had a feeling that could lead to only three scenarios.

Scenario One: she would enjoy all the pleasures of Riley as a lover, kiss him goodbye and move on, heart-whole.

Two: Riley would enjoy all the pleasures of *her* as a lover and leave her languishing when he tired of the affair.

Three: Riley would not tire of it and she would find herself irretrievably one of a twosome that could never become a threesome and she knew she could never give up her wish for a family.

One was improbable. Three, an outside chance but not worth the risk. Two was the most likely outcome and as the business with Riley was only a few days old, it wasn't too late to nip the whole thing in the bud.

But Riley didn't phone.

Customers phoned. Her mother phoned. The garage mechanic phoned to say that her van would not be ready until the next day. Pam phoned to say sorry and thanks and to tell her that Jeff's mother was talking to a counsellor and Savannah was doing so much better since she'd switched her to goat's milk and would she think they had a cheek if they asked another favour?

'You didn't exactly *ask* for the first one,' Alexandra pointed out, and set off a raft of apologies again.

'It's just that we're having Savannah christened and want you to be godmother. Please say yes. Jeff phoned Mr. Templeton this morning and asked if he would be godfather—'

Alexandra's heartbeat wavered then made up for the pause with a powerful surge that no doubt had some sensible, biological explanation.

'But he said no,' continued Pam mournfully. 'We did so want you both but I don't think he'll change his mind unless *you* can talk him into it. I wouldn't be game to pester him.'

'Why on earth should you think I could do that?' said Alexandra, but she smiled, relieved that she would not be losing touch with Brenna after all. 'I would be honoured to be Br— Savannah's godmother. By the way, who *was* the Riley on your note?'

'Riley?' said Pam, puzzled. 'Oh, you mean Kelly. Sean Kelly—he has the cleaning contract at the jazz club. I did some work for him before Savannah was born and he was so nice to me. I gave you his name in case you just couldn't look after Savannah, so that you wouldn't take her straight to the welfare people.'

'*Kelly?*' Alexandra took a deep breath. 'There was a distinct dot over the second letter. And those two 'ells' were totally different in size. I went to that club looking for a Riley.'

And found one.

'I always got into trouble for my handwriting at school, and besides I was upset when I wrote that. Sorry.' After a pause, she said, 'Oooh, you mean that's how you found Mr. Templeton? You mean, you've only known him for—four days?' There was a pause then, 'Wow!'

'There's no "wow" about it,' Alexandra said testily.

'I figured you must have known each other for ages. I mean, like—the way you argue and look at each other.'

'What way did we look at each other?' Alexandra demanded. 'No, never mind. When's the christening?'

Two hot, humid days later, Alexandra had concluded that none of her soul-searching had been necessary. Riley Templeton hadn't even made it to Scenario Two. He'd tired of the affair before it had even started. And the man had had the nerve to tell her to give Graham the big heave-ho in his favour.

When the phone rang near closing time, she answered it absently, her adolescent phone fixation over.

'Alexandra,' said Riley.

Her pulse beat took on a lively rhythm. She felt the prickle of heat renewed on her skin. She seized the nearest book and fanned her face with it.

'Oh—is that you, Riley?' As if anyone else had a voice quite like that.

'Your mother,' Riley said, with a kind of grittiness that suggested his teeth were clenched, 'is in my office...with *my* mother.'

'What...my *mother?*' Alexandra put down the book abruptly when she realised she was fanning her heated face with a copy of the Kama Sutra.

'She has been charged with a misdemeanour. She seems to be under the impression that, because she is painting my portrait, I am her legal representative. I am not. She has talked to the press and given my name as her counsel without my consent and connected me with the bloody *silliest*, adolescent piece of—' He took a deep breath. 'Get down here and take her home.'

Alexandra gaped. 'She phoned me earlier today and didn't say she was painting your portrait.'

'Maybe she thought it was irrelevant,' he snapped. 'I must have been out of my mind to agree. I should have known it would lead to more trouble because it is connected with *you*.'

'Oh, that's a bit unfair, Riley,' she protested, quickly doing the sums of a portrait sitting. Rhona liked three or four sittings for the preliminary sketches, then took up to six weeks to paint a portrait. How was she going to excise Riley from her life when her mother would be chatting about his three-quarter face potential, when there would be drawings of the man strewn from one end of her studio to the other for at least two months? And then there would be the finished portrait, a permanent record of Riley's passage through her life. Damn.

Belatedly she caught at one of his words. 'What do you mean, "misdemeanour"?'

'From now on, whenever anyone in your harebrained

family is accused of abduction or defacing public structures with graffiti please phone someone else.'

'Graffiti?' she bleated, snivelling in her seat as the bell jingled to mark the opening of the shop door. Graham came in wearing fluorescent lime Lycra bike pants, singlet and a helmet. His bike was visible through the window, leaning against the bench of 'bait' books displayed outside. He smiled at her and gently ran on the spot while he waited.

'Did you *hear* me?' Riley rapped in a voice that could splinter ice. 'I'll expect you in the next fifteen minutes.'

Distractedly she tidied her hair and explained to Graham that she had to close up now to go to the Inns of Court. Graham listened and nodded while he took his pulse. 'I've always wanted to meet your mother. Why don't I meet you there—could you bring my towel? I'll go the long way round of course, head up to the Terrace for some gradient work, just a warm-up for a distance cycle later—then—'

'Okay. See you there,' Alexandra cut in hastily, agreement the lesser of two evils. Distractedly, she sought out the towel, stuffed it in her bag before she locked up.

Rhona was in conversation with Riley's mother. Mrs. Templeton's patrician features were tinged with something very close to admiration. But it was clear that her feelings about Alexandra were still mixed. That was just because she was playing cupid in her son's affairs and any woman on the scene apart from Davina at present was likely to be viewed as an unnecessary distraction.

The door to Riley's office was ajar and Alexandra thought she caught the sound of shuffling paper through it. Her breasts tingled in the now familiar Pavlovian response.

'Oh, hello, Lexi,' her mother said, looking at her daughter and Graham, who had been chaining his bike to a parking sign outside the building when Alexandra arrived. 'Riley's washed his hands of me,' she said comfortably, confident she would be forgiven, in time. 'Can you give me a lift home?'

'No, I can't. The van's at the garage overnight.'

Alexandra fought to keep her eyes from the door to the inner sanctum. More paper sounds. Riley did not intend to come out, it seemed. 'Rhona—I don't understand what's happening. What did Riley mean by "graffiti"?'

'Oh, I wouldn't call it graffiti exactly,' Rhona said with a wave of the hand. 'Just a little—enhancement.'

'Enhancement of what?'

'A poster. Who's your friend?' Rhona asked, looking with interest at Graham.

Alexandra introduced them.

'I'm a great admirer of your work,' Graham told Rhona. 'Alexandra says that she hasn't your artistic genius or her father's, but I daresay the genes for it are merely unexpressed in her. Her progeny are sure to inherit your creative talent.'

Rhona blinked at this reassurance while Alexandra reflected that 'progeny' was probably even worse than 'offspring.'

No sooner had Graham's voice sounded than Riley's door opened and the man himself stood there, one hand on hip, the other clamped on the doorframe. He was in his shirt sleeves, his tie was missing, he'd been running his hands through his hair, and his jaw bore a suggestion of stubble.

Stay me with flagons, she thought. The man was gorgeous.

He'd come out to take a look at Graham, Alexandra decided as his eyes narrowed on Graham whose very nice, tanned muscles were sheened with perspiration. Riley had expected Graham to be worthy but inconspicuous—not this tall athlete with the Greek God looks. Notwithstanding all Graham's obvious assets *and* the

fact that he hadn't even bothered to phone her for two
days, Riley turned his gaze on Alexandra and let her see
his surprise that she had not yet given the man his
marching orders.

Gorgeous and arrogant. She could never get mixed up
with a man so convinced of his superiority. She gave
Riley a brilliant smile and made more introductions. The
two men shook hands in that measuring way men had
with each other, as if they were divining all kinds of
things from the pressure of the handshake. Riley surprised her by asking Graham about his cycling.

'In training for the Tri,' Graham told him. 'Triathlon.
I'm entered in the ''Hell of the West'' at Goondiwindi
in two weeks. A 750 metre swim, an 80K bike race and
a 20K run.'

'Poster?' she said to Rhona with one eye on Riley,
whose eyes were already glazing over at Graham's passion for detail. 'What poster?' And even as she said it,
she knew. 'Not that billboard of Gina Esposito on Milton
Road? Rhona! You didn't *write* anything on it, did you?'
she wailed, hoping for a beard and blacked-out teeth
rather than words. Rhona's words would be dynamite.
'And how did you reach it?' she added, remembering
the height and size of the billboard.

Rhona made some vague references to a friend of a
friend who had scaffolding and a truck. 'I wore overalls,'
she said. 'No one tried to stop me. I suppose everyone
thought I was a signwriter. Unfortunately, a police car
cruised by and—' She shrugged. 'Of course, the channel
soon heard about it and sent a camera out. I don't suppose it will get general coverage on television though,'
she said in an appeasing tone, glancing at Riley. 'After
all, the other channels won't want to give Channel
Three's current affairs program a plug, will they?'

Graham interrupted with a request for his towel. When
Alexandra produced it from the same large, patchwork
shoulder bag that had served as carry-all for baby sup-

plies, she saw Riley's eyebrows shoot up and his mouth quirk in amusement.

As the two older women and Graham drifted toward the elevator lobby, he moved alongside Alexandra and said in a low voice, 'Was *he* left on your doorstep, too?'

'A customer at the bookshop, actually,' she said coolly, objecting to the implication that Graham was just another stray she was mothering. 'The shop's on his running and bike route. I keep a towel at the shop for him.'

'And he pops in for a paperback and a quick wipe-down?' said Riley, making it sound positively salacious. 'I can't decide whether you've told him it's all over yet or not. You're probably too damned soft-hearted to make it decisive, and he's too busy assessing the lactic acid in his muscles to take a hint from anything less.'

'Told him what?' said Alexandra, opening her eyes wide.

Riley was at his most sardonic. 'Don't give me coyness, Alexandra. It's not your style.'

She gave a grimace of acknowledgement. 'All right, then. I haven't told him and it was only your brazen assumption that I would. If I *had* been intending to— tell him it's all over, I—had second thoughts.'

But they were about Riley and all on a warning note at that. His eyes narrowed again on Graham who had put on his bike helmet and was taking his pulse. 'I see.'

As he turned and strode into his office he said over his shoulder, 'I'll drive you and Rhona home.'

'Don't bother. We'll take a bus.'

But Rhona was already accepting the offer as a sign that she was forgiven, and Alexandra ground her teeth and went along only, she told herself, because she wanted to see what her mother had written on the billboard.

Alexandra was tense as they joined the traffic along Milton Road. She feared the ugly form that her mother's simmering hurt and rage might have taken. Desperately she hoped that Rhona had not scratched out the eyes of the smugly smiling image or torn chunks from those smooth, young cheeks. The press would have a field day with that...the jealous, ageing woman in a witchlike attack on her fair, young rival.

But what Rhona had done took her breath away. There were no crazed stabs or sweeps of paint. Gina Esposito's image was still lovely, still smiling. But it was an older image and the smile seemed no longer smug.

'Esposito,' Rhona said, almost to herself. 'Did you know that in ancient times people used to expose unwanted babies on the hillsides? Sometimes, in Italy, others would pick them up and give them a home and call them by the family name, or call them Esposito—the exposed one. The abandoned one.'

'Rhona—' Alexandra's voice cracked.

'I aged her a little,' Rhona said unnecessarily. 'To about forty-five. The age I was when he left me on a hillside.'

Alexandra was struck to the heart. The shadows under Gina's lovely brown eyes and in the smooth cheeks, the fine lines of living had been added subtly, even sympathetically.

'Funny how we women always hate the other woman when a man abandons us. We have to hate her because we can't stop loving him.' Rhona sighed. 'She probably thinks she'll never be abandoned, never get old, or if she does that she'll always be beautiful to him. *I* did.' Rhona looked up at her work. 'I'm doing Gina a favour, really. Reminding her.'

The traffic lights turned green. Alexandra took another look at the billboard in her rear-view mirror. The smug, air-brushed image on the poster had turned into a real woman and Rhona didn't hate her anymore.

'You must have been up on that scaffolding for ages.'

'Not long,' said Rhona with a faraway smile. 'From thirty to forty-five takes no time at all.'

There were students waiting for Rhona on her veranda. She hugged Alexandra, extracted a time from Riley for his next portrait sitting, and walked away like someone released from prison.

Long ago her lovely, talented, passionate mother had acted on impulse, been distracted by chemistry and loved a man who hadn't her own depths, and now she was alone. If she, Alexandra, needed something to strengthen her own resolution to avoid these pitfalls, then this was it. And somehow she *did* need something, always did, when Riley was around.

The man gave out some mysterious signals that seemed to jam her normal thought patterns. She was, even now, fielding perilous impulses to run fingertips over the crisply cut hair at the back of his neck, over that jaw with its hint of stubble. To button up his shirt. Or unbutton it. To let her hands cover his and travel with them as he put on his tie, his vest, his jacket, his robes. Or took them off.

Riley took his eyes from the road to glance at her, as if alerted by her covert attention. Alexandra flushed.

'Drop me in Elizabeth Street,' she said. 'I'll take a bus home.'

He ignored her completely and took the south-east freeway. A tape of piano music played loud enough to exclude conversation. Alexandra was tempted to ask him the name of the song he'd been playing in the club that night but thought better of it.

Riley took an exit from the freeway where the bike path from the city ended. Pedalling at a furious pace ahead of them, forcing the traffic wide around him, was a cyclist in fluorescent lime, his every muscle defined as he tackled the uphill slope.

'If it isn't Grover,' said Riley.

'Graham.' Alexandra glanced at her watch. 'Thirty-five minutes,' she commented. 'Graham will be pleased with that time.'

'Oh, this will be an interesting union,' Riley drawled. 'He'll run and you'll follow with his towel. Does he stop to take his pulse when you make love?'

'None of your business, Riley,' she told him coolly.

The traffic slowed to a crawl.

'So, he thinks your family's artistic genius will come out in your *progeny*,' he said with a hoot. He hadn't missed any of their conversation outside his office, she noted. 'What's he going to contribute apart from muscle?'

'Grit and determination, I should think,' she said, annoyed on Graham's behalf. Graham could be a bore at times but he was decent and dedicated to his own set of standards, qualities too often underrated. 'And he comes from quite an intellectual family. Graham thinks he and I could well produce another Einstein or Picasso.'

Riley snorted. He really seemed quite out of sorts.

'Not that I really care about genius,' Alexandra expanded, wondering if he could possibly be jealous. 'I've only ever wanted a bunch of nice, normal kids.'

Riley watched the cycle and its rider, still moving on the road shoulder while the cars halted.

'Maybe you should give a second thought to your second thoughts,' he said, as things got moving again.

Her heart pounded. Was Riley going to contest her decision? Would he try to persuade her? She hadn't counted on that.

'Why do you say that?'

Riley tooted the horn as they passed the toiling Graham in the surging, growling sports car.

'My antlers are bigger than his antlers,' he observed.

And of course, hearing that self-deprecating note in his voice she realized she was mistaken about his jealousy. Riley's tension had not been caused by her pairing herself off with Graham, but by all this talk of offspring. She was horrified by her insensitivity. She could only excuse it because, somehow, when she was with Riley he had such a powerful, earthy presence that she simply forgot he couldn't have children.

What could she say about such a lapse? Riley might think she was deliberately using his sterility just to score points. Alexandra found she quite desperately didn't want him to think badly of her. She looked at him, sympathy in her eyes, and could think of nothing that would not make it worse.

Alexandra thought about the kind of children he would have, if it were possible. She pictured some small, laughing versions of Riley. All children had trouble keeping their clothes on; Riley's children would probably be shedding them everywhere, following their father's example. She imagined a small girl with dark, blue eyes and a mop of uncontrollable curls, sitting on Riley's knee while he read to her... Alexandra bit her lip, aware that in her daydreams she had combined her genes with Riley's. And that was the only place they ever could combine.

In silence she sat beside him and wondered what a life without children would be like. If she had to live such a life, would she end up like Anna Brown, sneaking around with a baby basket, trying to steal a child to put in it?

But she would not have to live such a life.

The sports car swooped into her drive and came to a throbbing standstill. Riley engaged the brake and turned to her. He looked stern and shuttered, but she felt she was seeing the calm surface over stormy depths. Dismayed by her insensitivity, she was especially warm to Riley when she said goodnight. Never again, she vowed, would she raise the subject of children.

She even leaned over and kissed him on the cheek. 'Thanks for helping Rhona, Riley. And for driving us

home.' Her lips brushed his cheek again, closer to his
mouth. She drew back a fraction and smiled up at him.
'You're a lovely man.'

Just what there was about that to make his nostrils
flare she couldn't say. Riley took in a sharp breath,
seized her by the shoulders and kissed her full on the
mouth as if seeking to erase those friendly goodnight
kisses. This was a red-blooded affair, his mouth demanding entrance, his tongue probing the inner warmth
of her, provoking her response.

She kissed him back, pressed past the painful barrier
of the gearstick, to clasp his fabulous shoulders, slid her
hands under his jacket so that only his shirt was between
her skin and his. And that was too great a barrier.
Feverishly, she pulled at the shirt-tails, rumpled them up
so that her palms spread on his bare back. She was fum-
bling for his belt buckle when Riley suddenly leaned
back and gripped her wrists, firmly impelled her back
into her seat.

He picked up her spectacles that had slipped, unnot-
iced to the floor, and handed them to her.

'Goodnight, Alexandra,' he said with a certain glinting satisfaction as he noted the tremor in her hand as
she took the glasses.

His car reversed from the driveway, whirled into the
road. There was a squeal of brakes as he cornered, then
he was gone. Alexandra touched her lips with a fingertip.
'I must not fall in love with Riley,' she muttered, as she
walked across her front lawn.

She checked down under the front steps as she had
ever since the night she'd found Brenna there. Nothing.

One of Sam's goats bleated. The frog across the road
croaked at nine-second intervals.

'I must not fall in love with Riley,' she said again.

In Alexandra's mind, some elusive notes of music
played and her mind toyed briefly with the notion that

she was too late rehearsing those particular words. She managed to suppress the last, but not the music.

And like his signature tune, Riley lingered. If only she could think of the name of the melody, Alexandra thought, she might get it out of her mind, and Riley with it. But no name came to her. The music and Riley stayed.

Riley's gaze was fixed murderously on the truck in front of him. It was piled high with watermelons barely restrained within a double rail. Fortunately for the melons and unfortunately for him, the truck was travelling at a snail's pace.

'A lovely man,' he said between clenched teeth. 'A lovely man!'

If ever there was a phrase that had a 'but' to follow, that was one. Alexandra was giving him compensation prizes now. Which meant she knew. Riley's stomach churned. How the hell had he let this happen? He was old enough and experienced enough not to put himself in the way of humiliation again. It was bad when Davina had burst his bubble all those years ago but at least he'd had the excuse of youth and inexperience on his side. This time he'd known from the start that he shouldn't get involved. For God's sake, Alexandra had told him, actually *told* him, that she didn't want him except to find her foundling's mother.

That was his mistake. Sheer ego. She had not been impressed with his piano playing and he'd wanted to impress her. She had told him that ludicrous story about Bernadette St. John, just so that she could sever all connection with him. And he had convinced himself that she was just playing hard to get, seen it as a challenge. Damned fool that he was, he had confidently rushed to meet it, not realizing that he was already in trouble.

'Damn you—at least pull over to the side and let me

pass!' Riley sounded the horn. The truck continued at a
leisurely pace.

Alexandra and the way she looked at him sometimes.
Compassionate. His knuckles whitened on the steering
wheel and the idea of Alexandra's pity. But that had to
be it. She knew he was more than halfway in love with
her and being the kind of woman she was, she didn't
want to hurt his feelings. He blasted the horn twice.

'Get out of my way!'

This was preposterous. He'd met her less than a week
ago. He was no green boy to be stricken, and by a
woman with freckles, glasses and an undergraduate taste
in clothes. Yet he couldn't even remember this degree
of desolation when Davina had told him she was leaving.
His pride had been battered. He had been forced to re-
draft his own image of himself as an unsuspecting, conceited fool. But he didn't remember feeling this way—
as if his life had just changed permanently for the worse.

'Will you move over?' He glared at the watermelons.

Alexandra could turn her back on the amazing chemistry they generated, the chemistry she openly admitted
existed between them, in favour of that running, jumping
and cycling freak.

And yet. Riley reviewed his memory of the sight and
sound and feel of Alexandra in his arms. Perhaps he was
being defeatist. There had to be more than just lust to
prompt a woman like Alexandra to make love on a
man's desk.

As he recalled it, his confidence returned. Oh, yes. She
might claim to dismiss chemistry, she might *intend* to
resist it, but when put to the test Alexandra Page had
been unable to do either. Riley's eyes narrowed. He had
formed a healthy respect for Alexandra's strength of pur-
pose and tenacity in the short time he'd known her, so
it was revealing that in this, she failed and kept on failing.

Tonight, for instance. Treating him like a nice, big

brother with those chaste pecks on the cheek, but the moment he touched her, she'd gone up in flames. If he hadn't stopped her, she would have had his belt undone and been going for his zip. Riley dwelt on this fact with a certain regret for missed opportunity, but renewed optimism. Now, now, don't go getting cocksure, Templeton. He grinned.

His eyes narrowed on the loaded truck and his brain began to work again. Riley reviewed and calculated his chances and decided that some improvisation was necessary. He tapped out a rhythm on the steering wheel, hummed a few notes. Time to change his tune, he decided, if he wanted her. And afterwards he would probably find this fascination with her wasn't anything but a pleasurable, passing fancy. Riley felt quite cheered.

The truck moved over onto the unsealed shoulder of the road and Riley drove past. Of course, if it was just lust on his part, why had he stopped her tonight?

A bump in the surface jolted the truck and a watermelon fell over the side and smashed to a pink pulp on the road. The bigger they are, the harder they fall, thought Riley.

CHAPTER NINE

IT WAS a fine, early February day for the christening. The church was weatherboard, tiny, perched on a grassy slope bobbing with dandelions.

'We may be the only ones who come,' Alexandra said to Sam as they got out of the *Volumes* van. She leaned in for her broad-brimmed Italian straw hat. One of the tiny, dried flowers trimming it fell off and she brushed it away. 'Pam's family live in South Australia and Jeff's might not turn up.'

But they weren't the only ones. A man strode through the long grass, taking a short cut towards them. A tall, dark-haired, wide-shouldered man wearing sunglasses and a dazzling white shirt under a blazer.

Sam was delighted. 'If it isn't my old mate, Riley,' he said. There was some mutual back-slapping. 'Come round for a beer before I go to Melbourne? You can tune my piano.'

'What are you doing here?' said Alexandra ungraciously, their last farewell looming large in her mind. Riley, stopping her from practically ripping off his trousers. She knew he was looking her over but she could only look into the blank dark glasses. She slapped her hat against her thigh. A couple of blooms shot from the dried flower trim.

'I'm the godfather,' he said in a Marlon Brando voice that set Sam chuckling.

'I thought you refused that honour.'

'So did I,' he said dryly. 'I allowed myself to be—persuaded.'

So, Pam and Jeff had found the nerve to pester Riley, after all. Several dried flower heads flew outward.

'Nobody told me you'd changed your mind.'

The dark lenses tilted in another scrutiny. 'You seem quite agitated, Alexandra. Is it because you and I are about to become godparents?' His blank gaze appeared to fix on her hat as it shed more blooms. 'We should hurry. The subtractions are coming thirty seconds apart.'

Alexandra looked down at the hat with its depleted trim.

'Oh, very funny.'

He smirked. In irritation, she stepped closer and whipped off his sunglasses. But though she got a close-up of heart-stopping dark blue eyes, she could divine nothing there but a sort of boyish glee at his own wit. Just what she had expected, she couldn't have said. His eyebrows went up mockingly.

'Don't like sunglasses, Alexandra?'

'It's bad manners to keep them on when you're talking to someone,' she said, thrusting them at him. 'The other person can't see your eyes, but you can see theirs.'

'You think that's taking unfair advantage?' He folded the glasses, slipped them into his blazer pocket. 'You know how I feel about using one's advantages, Alexandra.'

The last time he'd said that, she'd been sprawled half-naked on his desk. Alexandra fanned herself with the hat, then, catching Riley's amused gaze on the flowers flying from it, plonked it on over her frizzing French roll and stuffed some stray strands of hair under the brim.

Sam went on ahead and they followed him along the path beaten by the faithful.

There was something very strange about standing at the font, in church beside Riley, making solemn responses to the clergyman. Something decidedly intimate about posing for Pam's photographs, the baby in her arms, Riley's arm around her waist. Something very odd about seeing their signatures together on the baptismal records.

She nearly made a joke of it. Nearly said, 'Look, your name's on the note with mine, again.' It hadn't been his the first time but now it was. They were being written into each other's life histories.

Jeff's parents turned up, after all. His mother seemed the calmer for therapy but hardly ever took her eyes off Savannah. His father hardly ever took his eye from the viewfinder on his video. After the christening, on the neutral territory of Alexandra's back garden, with its unfinished brick paths and tubs of herb cuttings and seedlings, peace broke out as a more confident Pam put the baby in Anna Brown's arms.

'I know you don't like the name we gave her,' she said to her husband's mother. 'But when she's older, it's bound to be shortened. Already we call her Anna sometimes.'

The woman looked astonished, as if she'd never recognised her own name in the despised one. Alexandra decided that there was more to Pam than met the eye.

'I see that Gina Esposito has decided not to take legal action against your mother,' Riley said, ably assisting her to set out sandwiches and mini-pizzas on a table on her remaining patch of lawn.

'She ought to send Rhona a big, fat cheque to cover the fine, considering the publicity she's got out of it.'

The business of the billboard had, predictably, not been featured on any but the Channel Three news but it had been picked up by the newspapers. The 'matured' picture of Gina had appeared several times and stimulated a flow of letters on the subject of men with Peter Pan complexes, and the dearth of older women on television. Channel Three current affairs had never rated so well.

'Have you seen Rhona's sketches yet?' Riley asked. 'Of me?'

'I never see anything until Rhona's finished a portrait,' she told him. 'She doesn't like me to look.'

Riley was sceptical. 'You mean, if you visit and there's something on the easel, you can resist walking around to see what it is?'

Alexandra shrugged. 'Rhona doesn't like me to look, so I don't and won't. Not even sketches of you,' she said ironically.

'I'm impressed. Two women in one family who mind their own business.'

'How *is* your mother?' Alexandra enquired, realizing too late how it sounded.

Riley gave a huff of laughter. 'Rhona thinks my mother wants to organise everything and everyone because she's a frustrated lawyer.'

'Why didn't she study law?'

He looked startled. 'Who, Mum?'

'Weren't all her family lawyers?'

'The men were.'

'But the girls went to good schools and learned how to be supportive wives to men who were lawyers,' finished Alexandra. 'Maybe she should go to law school now.'

'Who, Mum?' he said again.

'If you insist on thinking of her only as your mother, then you can't complain if she keeps mothering you,' she said tartly.

Riley acknowledged that with a frown. 'She would think she's too old to go back to school,' he said at last.

Alexandra shrugged. 'She'll never be younger.'

Riley thought about it, then gave her a slow-burning smile. 'Why is it that I feel like I'm wearing blinkers when I'm not around you?'

Why was it that she felt she needed them when she was around him? Alexandra looked in his eyes and felt the charge of awareness through to the soles of her feet.

What were those words she had rehearsed? I must not fall in love with Riley.

'Is Graham coming?' he asked.

'He's in Goondiwindi for the "Hell of the West."'

'Ah, that's right. You must miss him. Have you set a date yet?'

Alexandra was unsettled. She grew evasive, guilty that she had allowed this fiction to go on. Not that it hurt anyone exactly, but she felt she was somehow using Graham even if only in name. Yet the idea of admitting to Riley that Graham was, and never would be, any more than a friend, made her feel unaccountably vulnerable. Also, where had Riley's sarcasm gone? He had asked the question quite casually, as if the answer didn't matter to him at all.

Sam bade them turn around for his camera at that moment and she managed a smile without having to answer.

'He's a terrific guy,' Riley resumed, after they had posed for the snap.

She looked sharply at him. 'I thought you didn't like him.'

'What gave you that idea?'

Suspiciously she studied him. 'Maybe all those snide comments. All that sarcasm.'

Riley thrust his mouth forward in an almost Gallic expression of regret. 'Sarcasm is an occupational hazard. No, I think you and Graham will make a great team.'

And that was the second time he'd got Graham's name right. Why did that annoy her?

'You look beautiful today, Alexandra,' he said, studying her thoroughly as if she were a courtroom exhibit. His right index finger followed the strap of her flowered dress in an absent gesture of appreciation. She felt The Chill down her spine and hoped Riley's eagle eye would not spot the goose flesh on her arms.

'Thanks,' she said huskily. Beautiful? She wasn't, and

had never expected to hear Riley say it. Come to think of it, she hadn't seen Riley in quite this mood before. Beautiful, he called her, but so casually that she couldn't find any meaning in it. It occurred to her that she had, from the start, felt special to Riley. Not beautiful. Special. She felt let down and strove for a cheerfulness that came out too heartily.

'How do you like the herb garden? It's almost finished.'

He breathed deeply of the herb-scented air and gazed around with obvious pleasure at the garden beds, some planted with thyme and rhubarb and rosemary and some dug-over and still awaiting planting, at Sam's best milker staring over the side fence, at the generous wire-netting enclosure with its grapevine, where chickens pecked and plok-plokked.

'I like it,' he said and smiled down at her. His dark-lashed eyes crinkled at the corners. 'No sundial yet?'

'I've seen plenty,' she told him. Damn, but he was gorgeous, and he was just making small talk. I must not fall... 'But I'm holding out for something special.'

'I know just what you mean,' said Riley.

There were champagne toasts and more photographs, more cosy godparents-with-godchild scenes enacted for the video and the several cameras present. Would these photographs of her and Riley end up in her photo albums, the only trace, after all, of their odd relationship? It was exactly how she knew it had to be, yet she had a sudden depressing vision of one day looking at these pictures of herself with the tall, vital man with ruffled hair and saying, 'He was just someone I used to know.'

Sam kept the wineglasses topped up and Pam handed around the sandwiches and cakes that she and Alexandra had made earlier.

'You must tell Alexandra the name of that song,' Pam said rather nervously to Riley as she offered a platter to him. 'She was humming it all morning, said she couldn't get it out of her mind.'

Alexandra wasted a repressive look on Pam.

'You were playing it in the Blue Parrot the night you met, she said,' Pam went on breathlessly, making it sound as if she and Alexandra had shared giggling, high-school confidences.

Alexandra shrugged, trying to dampen the effect. 'Isn't it annoying when a tune gets inside your head and you can't stop it? You wake up at night and it goes round and round and you *know* that you know the name of it but it's always just out of reach.'

She looked over at Riley then and was shaken by the sudden heat he was generating. What had she said? Alexandra reviewed her last words and could find nothing to put that sexy, come-to-bed look in Riley's eyes. For heaven's sake, anyone would think she'd been quoting from the Kama Sutra.

'A mind worm, I think it's called.'

'A what worm?'

'Mind worm—when the same phrase of music or some words of a song keep winding through your mind no matter what you do.'

She had used the humdrum image of a worm deliberately to wipe that disturbing glitter from his eyes. And gratifyingly it appeared to work. Riley stopped looking as if he wanted to ravish her on the spot and became the life and soul of the party. He took off his blazer and swapped jokes with Sam. He rolled up his sleeves and made himself indispensable pouring drinks and handing around trays of food.

He took off his tie and tendered the big, honey bear to a cross-eyed Savannah, sang the Winnie-the-Pooh song from behind the tartan-ribboned teddy to the mystified child. Alexandra marvelled that this was the same man who had been so grumpy when she'd discovered the cuddly toy in his car.

It was all being faithfully recorded on Mr. Brown's video.

With his eye to the viewfinder, Mr. Brown backed onto the garden and got his camera strap tangled in the herbs. The fragrance of rosemary teased at Alexandra's nostrils as she stood in the sun watching Riley with his arms full of baby and honey bear. He sang softly and seemed to shield the infant with a strength that was curbed to gentleness. Tears sprang to her eyes.

This was the picture that she had always carried in her mind. A goal to aim for. A man of strength who knew how to use it, a child on his knee, and her, Alexandra, watching over them. And ironically, seeing the real thing in front of her made her mind picture fuzz at the edges. She stood very still and tried to get it back the way it had always been, like a promise of the future. With a sense of panic she pursued it but could not make it clear again.

One small bit of red, mixed in by chance and painted over again and again, would remain and influence the final picture.

Nearly two hours later, Riley left without taking any more clothes off. And he still hadn't told Alexandra the name of that song.

Time passed. Savannah's gums swelled and Pam phoned regularly to keep Alexandra informed as to the eruption of her first tooth. Alexandra, helped by Sam, laid some more bricks on her herb garden paths and planted sorrel, dill and mint. Sam, helped by Alexandra, found his old military uniform and took some nips and tucks in it for the reunion.

The book about St. Bernadette sold. The Rev. W. Morley Punshon's *Sermons* didn't. Alexandra put it out front on the customer 'bait' table.

The frog in the lily pond across the road fell silent.

She saw Riley on television, fleetingly, in his robes in

a story about a man he'd successfully prosecuted and who had since been beaten up in jail. The man's relatives scowled and shook their fists at the cameras.

Riley would soon move out of his wrecked apartment and the renovators would move in. She knew this from Rhona, who absently passed along tantalizingly incomplete bits of conversation exchanged with him in his sittings.

'I wonder,' Rhona said once as Alexandra roamed around the studio failing to come across any of the preliminary drawings that usually cluttered the place before her mother started painting a portrait. 'This ex-wife, Davina—'

Alexandra was used to Rhona's disjointed conversation but she waited with mounting frustration. 'Yes, yes—' she urged. 'What about Davina?'

Rhona chewed on the end of a brush. 'I think Fiona shouldn't try so hard to matchmake,' she said at last. More chewing and consideration. 'Riley doesn't like being pushed. He seems very fond of Davina's little boys. If Fiona left him alone, he might even...'

The sleepwalker's look was in her eyes and Alexandra knew she would never get her mother to finish the thought. As if she needed to. Pretty obvious that Riley had been seeing Davina again.

Davina and her ready-made family. That probably explained that odd change of mood of his at the christening. He'd indulged in a mild flirtation with Alexandra, would have indulged in a brief affair if it had not been for her own caution. And, she added honestly, if it had not been for his mobile phone and his mother.

But that had been just a bit of fun on the side. Davina and her boys was serious stuff.

In the first week of March Sam flew to Melbourne for his reunion. One of his goat-breeding friends had arrived in a truck and taken Sam's goats away for a fortnight.

Sam left her a small token of his affection at her back door.

Thinking it was a bag of Sam's plums, she picked it up and broke out in a sweat when it cried 'Mama.' There were some plums in the bag, along with a cutely smiling Mama doll.

It was the unnatural quiet that woke Alexandra the first night of her neighbour's absence. No frog. No goats. Just the occasional snap and creak of the tin roof, a dog barking somewhere, the hum of the freeway carried in waves on a breeze.

It was two-thirty in the morning, the time when the mind was most vulnerable to the dreaded mind worm. The music started in her head, just the first eight bars, over and over. She hummed 'God Save the Queen' but even that stately piece of music didn't drive it out. At length, she got up and filled the kettle, picked a few mint leaves from the pot on her sill and dropped them in a cup. Idly, she screwed the top off the honey jar and pulled aside the curtain, peered outside.

A light flickered. Vanished. Alexandra shrugged, was about to turn away to spoon honey in with the mint when it appeared again, as the breeze shifted the clump of banana palms that normally prevented her seeing the window of Sam's spare bedroom. He must have been rummaging for some piece of memorabilia to take with him this morning, and left the light on.

She set down the honey jar and licked some of the stickiness from her hand as she went to fetch the spare keys Sam left with her. The night air hinted at autumn and there was a spattering of rain in the breeze, so she put on her gardening shoes and dragged on her old trench coat over her nightshift. Leaving her exterior light on, she ventured out the back door, across the fence and over Sam's paddock, lighting her way with a torch.

Perhaps, while she was here, she would check the stove and appliances in case Sam had forgotten to turn other switches off. He was seventy-five, she reminded herself. It was with a vague sense of disloyalty to him that she unlocked the back door and walked through the house, guided by the overflow of light.

She glimpsed miniature train tracks on the floor as she planted her hand flat on the door and went in.

A near-naked man crouched on the floor.

Alexandra recoiled, raised the torch above her head as adrenalin pumped through her bloodstream. Even before he turned to look over his shoulder she had recognised the back of his neck and the thick, dark hair. And the topography of that broad, bare back was familiar territory in a tactile rather than a visual sense. She froze in attack mode.

Riley grinned up at her. 'Neighbourhood Watch?' he enquired.

'What—' she began. She lowered the potential blunt instrument. 'Why—'

Riley turned back to the tiny train tracks and fiddled with something she couldn't see. The muscles of his back twitched and rippled. He wore some cotton knit pyjama pants in an unlikely shade of purple. Hunkered down as he was, the pants pulled tight over a splendid backside revealing a long length of spine and two indents either side of it. Purple. She couldn't take her eyes off the colour.

'What are you doing here, Riley?'

But at that moment a model train engine charged out along the track and Riley gave a whoop of triumph.

'It's—after two in the morning,' she went on, feeling as if she'd strayed down a rabbit hole. Perhaps this was another of those dreams that always seemed to feature Riley in various states of undress. 'What are you *doing* here?'

The engine hurtled into a curve and fell off the track, lay with wheels whirring. Riley picked it up and bent over it, giving the wheels his fullest attention.

'We'll soon fix that,' Riley muttered. Then he stood up.

'I'm staying here,' he told her. If the back view of naked torso and clinging purple pants was revealing, the front was almost indecent. 'The question is, Alexandra my love, what are you doing here…and in your nightie, too?'

He smiled warmly and, put off by that casual 'my love' and the intimate drape of purple, knitted cotton over masculine attributes, she let him gawp for several moments at the diaphanous nightshift before she dragged the trench coat edges together.

'You can't be staying here,' she said flatly.

'I've moved in while Sam's away. The insurance company's paid up at last and the renovators have moved into my place. It's chaos.'

Alexandra's gaze flitted around the room, avoiding Riley himself who seemed to be occupying more than his share of space, with his big shoulders extended in a hands-on-hips pose.

'He didn't say anything about you moving in,' she challenged, moving about Sam's cluttered shelves of old magazines, records and odds and ends.

'You won't get me on a break-and-enter charge,' Riley said, and there was a grittier sound in his voice now. 'Sam gave me his keys. You want to see them?' He patted nonexistent pockets on his lean hips, drawing her gaze back to the fascinating combination of flesh tones and purple. And dark chest hair in an arrowhead shape that trickled into a line that vanished beneath the purple. 'Don't have them on me at this moment,' he murmured with a hint of a smirk as he saw he had her complete attention.

Alexandra turned away and hurried through the house, Sam's spare keys jingling in her hand.

'Sorry. I just thought Sam had left a light on by accident, that's all, and came over to check it out. Sam leaves a set of spare keys with me in case he ever locks himself out. Neighbours tend to do that around here.' Riley followed her, his big feet padding on the floor-boards. It was, she thought with an irrational stab of panic, like being stalked by one of the big cats. She speeded up.

'All this warm spirit of community is quite a novelty to someone like me, used to an impersonal apartment block.'

She had reached the back door where she'd come in and went at it frantically to get it open. The torch and the keys got in the way and as she fumbled, Riley leaned across her from behind and turned the handle.

Her trench coat was old but good and had a fifteen-year guarantee to keep out rain, winds and chill. It was useless against heat. Riley's body exuded a midsummer heat, his bare arm remained raised to the latch, giving off a soapy scent that was a potent mix of just-bathed child overlaid with the lusty smell of adult male. So close was his arm to her face that she had only to turn her head to lay her mouth against sleek skin over flexed muscle.

She dropped the small bunch of spare keys and dived for them. Riley got to them first, casually hemming her in against the door as they stood again.

'Um—perhaps you should keep them,' she said, fixing her eyes firmly on the keys. It was darker here but not dark enough. 'You might not like the idea of someone else having keys. You might not feel—'

'Safe?' he prompted, leaning in very close. 'What is that scent on you?' Riley sniffed delicately at her temple, nosed in under her ear for another deep breath. 'Mmmm. Don't tell me, let me guess—'

She couldn't have told him anyway because she couldn't think as Riley murmured guesses and sniffed and plucked aside, with finger and thumb, the large collar of her coat to investigate the shoulder it exposed.

'Not rosemary...' he said in a low, amused voice. 'I'd remember that. Mmmm—you always smell so—good.' Her quick surge of pleasure vanished as he added, 'Not *medicinal* exactly, but something that's bound to be good for you.'

Alexandra grasped the collar, made an effort to restore order, but Riley seized her by the waist in a sudden, boyish spasm. Rainproof fabric rustled as it was crushed beneath his hands.

'Mint!' he exclaimed, looking down at her with a triumph quite out of proportion, she felt. 'You've been handling mint.'

'Oh, yes,' she croaked. 'That's right. I had just crushed some leaves to make mint tea when I saw the light.' Alexandra felt his hold relax and she summoned up her resolve to make a dash for it.

'Mint tea,' said Riley appreciatively. His grip firmed. 'But not just mint,' he said, his brow furrowed. He rechecked her temples and under her jaw and the lobe of her ear, sniffing like a wine connoisseur who goes back for another taste to refresh his memory. 'There's something else—'

At length, he gave a last, bloodhound sniff and lifted the keys that he had retrieved, tapped an index finger stickily to the ring. 'Honey?' he enquired.

'Oh. Mmmm.'

He took her hand, raised it, turned it over and touched his tongue to the ball of her thumb. She shivered in the coat that was guaranteed to keep out chills. The small, moist point of contact delivered powerful sensations to the rest of her body. Alexandra made a tiny sound, closed her eyes involuntarily.

'Yes, it is honey,' Riley confirmed cheerfully, and stood aside to let her go. When she didn't immediately follow suit, he took her gently, but impersonally, by the shoulders and shifted her aside, opened the door.

'I can see I'll have to get used to these neighbourly

ways.' He gave her the keys. 'You keep the spares for Sam's house as usual.' Riley's smile was neighbourly. So was the brisk little pat to her shoulder. 'After all, Sam's got yours. Or rather, I have.'

Alexandra left.

'Can I drop by sometime to pick some of your mint?' he called after her. 'I like the sound of mint tea.'

Alexandra gave a noncommittal wave of one hand without looking back. Two weeks of Riley as a neighbour? Riley, in her garden, picking herbs? She slithered over the fence beneath the plum trees, roundly cursing Sam and the mysteries of mateship that could make such instant buddies of Riley and her elderly neighbour.

'You could at least have *warned* me, Sam,' she muttered.

Inside, she wriggled out of the coat, tossed it on its peg by the back door. 'And *you* were completely useless,' she accused the coat that was proof against just about everything but Riley Templeton.

Sam phoned her from Melbourne the next day and she took up her grievance with him. 'You found time to play a stupid practical joke, but didn't tell me that Riley was going to stay in your house.'

Sam gave an evil chuckle. 'You found the plums then? I left you a note with them.'

'There was no note. I can't believe you never even spoke to me about it, Sam.'

'I left it sticking out from under the mat, so you couldn't miss it,' he said. 'And I don't have to get your permission, girlie, to let a friend stay in my own home.'

Ruefully, she found herself making a rare apology to her neighbour. Riley had a bad effect on her, in more ways than one. She looked down at the palm of her hand as if she might read there a chemical trace of Riley then closed her fist over it. No more neighbourly little *tête a tête*s with Riley with his sexy hide and purple Daks. Without even trying he chipped away at her resolution.

The next evening, she slipped over and left a large bunch of mint on his front doorstep where he couldn't miss it. Alexandra felt she had struck just the right note. Neighbourly, but making a return visit by Riley unnecessary. Of course, if Riley wanted to knock on her door, nothing would stop him.

But apparently he didn't want to.

It was Saturday, three days after he had arrived, before she saw him again. In the meantime she had seen his car come and go, the houselights switch on and off and once had caught a drift of crackling jazz music before the volume was turned down.

Riley just turned up when she was working in her garden, digging out a shallow trench to extend her path, shovelling sand and levelling it. Hot and sweaty, coated in sand and dirt, she loaded recycled bricks into the wheelbarrow and was halfway to the laying site before she saw him. The barrow wobbled, nearly overset the load.

'The wheel's loose,' she explained, dragging a dirty forearm across her face.

'I'll fix it for you tomorrow,' said Riley. 'Like a cool drink?'

Riley set down a jug and two glasses on the grass and gestured for her to join him.

'That's very thoughtful, Riley.'

'Neighbourly,' he corrected. 'Besides, I'm hoping to borrow some books. Sam's run to only two topics—war and goats.' He patted the grass beside him.

She hesitated. He wore denim cut-offs and trainers and a faded khaki T-shirt that cherished every beautiful contour of his chest and shoulders. Riley's jaw bristled with an overnight beard but his hair was damp, as if from the shower, and she caught a drift of that potent smell that reminded her of baby and full-grown man all at once.

He handed her a frosted glass that clinked with ice

cubes and smiled when she hesitated. 'It's genuine—not Sam's trick glass that pours water down your front. I picked it up by mistake in the middle of the night and got soaked.'

To take her mind off Riley, wet to the skin in purple pyjama pants, she sat down and told him about Sam's more original practical jokes.

'He grows different varieties of pumpkins and once he left one at my door. When I picked it up, this voice whispered 'I'm a Queensland Blue.' He'd rigged up a radio speaker inside it and lurked under the plum trees with a transmitter. At first I thought the bundle under the stairs was one of Sam's pranks. But the joke was on me.'

Riley looked thoughtfully at his drink. 'I rather thought it was on me,' he murmured, then went on quickly. 'If you still want a sundial, I can show you one you might like. Got an hour to spare next Saturday?'

They agreed on a time a week ahead and drifted inside where Riley browsed her shelves while she washed her hands. They went down-under to sift through her excess stock stored in boxes, passing each other titles that recalled childhood and school, holidays and solitary adult times, recommending stories that they somehow knew the other would like, reading out loud a few lines here and there that had lived on in their memories.

It was fine until Riley had culled his choices to a short-list and picked up book after book, letting the pages flutter past his fingers. Alexandra crossed her arms across her chest and thought what bad luck it was that she, a bookseller, had to associate that particular sound with this particular sensation and this particular man.

Loaded with books, the jug and glasses, Riley headed for the fence.

'You haven't forgotten the CUFF dinner next Saturday?'

She stared. 'But—surely—you were just proving a point.'

Riley's smile neither confirmed nor denied it. 'I've bought the tickets now. Don't let me down.' A pause. 'Will Graham mind?'

Alexandra felt that she was venturing onto that jungle path, but the power to resist had dwindled. 'Graham has—um—left his towel at the boutique next door to the bookshop,' she said.

Riley's eyes glittered. 'That's all right, then. It's at the Heritage. Formal wear, I'm afraid.'

He went and she put on her work gloves and went back to work, refusing to watch him make his way across the paddock. But in her mind she had a picture of him, at his ease on her sun-dappled grass, long legs crossed at the ankles and a smile in his eyes. *Oh, he was just a man I used to know.*

But with a kind of gathering resignation, she accepted that it was way too late already and she would never be able to say quite that about him.

In spite of herself, she felt a buzz of anticipation at the idea of going out with Riley, being seen with him as his partner. *Formal wear, I'm afraid.* Her eyes sparkled. Did that mean he thought she had nothing to wear? That her penchant for baggy pants and shirts and long skirts meant she never wore anything else?

Alexandra quickly reviewed and rejected anything formal hanging in her wardrobe. On Monday she would have to slip into the boutique next door where Graham now left his towel.

Riley took to Sam's place, and to hers, with enthusiasm. In the late dusk of several evenings, he could be seen chugging around Sam's paddock on the rider mower, cutting swathes around trees and several pieces of rusting farm machinery. When it got dark, she could hear him tuning Sam's piano, playing the same note over and over until one night she went over to beg him to change to another. She ended up having dinner with him and, afterwards, poring over Sam's piano strings with him.

Riley turned up one morning, dressed for work, as she made for the chicken run to collect eggs. 'I've never done that,' he said with what she could only call a wistful expression.

'What—no comics in the house? And no chooks in the backyard? What a deprived childhood you've had.' She grinned and waved him in, the best dressed visitor the chooks had ever had.

With boyish zest he searched for the eggs, and put each find in the basket on her arm, saying, 'One for Mr. Hawkins. One for you. And another for Mr. Hawkins...'

The following Saturday Riley directed Alexandra to a rambling demolition site and used a key to unlock the high security fence around it.

'The developer is a former client of mine,' Riley told her after she had driven the van inside. 'One of the grateful ones.' As they passed a once-grand old house, smashed into a pile of rubble, he added, 'Thank God. If he'd been dissatisfied think what a mess *he* could have made of my apartment.'

He guided her to a rubbish-strewn wilderness of parched canna lilies and rampant morning glory vine. They got out of the van. 'Somewhere in here, he said,' Riley muttered, dragging great drifts of vine aside to reveal a stone sundial.

Alexandra knelt beside it, ran fingers over the chipped, hand-carved stone that was caked in dried mud. 'It looks as if it was in hiding, waiting to be rescued,' she said with a laugh and looked up at Riley. 'I love it.'

'Are you sure you love it—or do you just feel sorry for it?' he said rather crisply.

'Does it matter? I want it, so—how much is it? And can we take it home now?'

'Oh, you *want* it,' he muttered. 'That's something else again.'

But their new sense of friendship transcended the odd little exchange and they took the sundial home, wrapped in a blanket, and spent hours scraping it clean and setting it in its new garden bed. Keen to see the overall result, Alexandra ceremoniously laid the last brick on her herb garden path as the late afternoon sun began to fade.

'Finished,' she said, smiling.

And when she looked at Riley she knew it was true. They could do no more. Sam's grass was cut, the model train was running again, the piano was tuned, the wheelbarrow was fixed, her paths were laid, her spare stock sorted, the sundial in place. They had rushed from distraction to distraction but suddenly there was just the two of them, neighbours, friends... 'I'll call for you at seven,' said Riley, smiling at her with more than neighbourly friendship in his dark eyes. He reached out and his fingers stopped just short of touching. They sketched a delicate, caressing motion that followed the shape of her tangled hair. 'Wear your hair loose? Please.'

She wore her hair loose with an ankle-length charcoal shift with thin straps. It scooped low over her breasts and clung silkily to her hips and mysteriously made her skin look paler, her hair redder and her legs longer. Around her neck she fastened a smooth circlet of silver, made by one of Rhona's designer friends. Alexandra rubbed in a little of the aromatic oil she used in place of perfume. It was musk, earthy and powerful and a deliberate departure from her usual preferences.

She met Riley on her front veranda. His steps slowed on the stairs when he saw her. His long, slow scrutiny was gratifyingly appreciative.

Last glimpsed in dirty shorts and T-shirt, Riley himself was a sight to behold in a tucked, white shirt, white dinner jacket and a black bow tie. This was not fair, she thought. Dinner jackets had been especially designed to make ordinary men look extraordinary; men who looked like Riley should be banned from wearing them under a law of unfair advantage.

The dinner was a splendid affair in a room overlooking the river. Mrs. Templeton was resplendent in ivory satin and pearls. It might have been because she was so busy with committee responsibilities that she greeted Alexandra with a sort of philosophical acceptance. On the other hand it might have been because Davina was there, too, blond and elegant, with a possessive, prosperously built man.

'I won't pretend. I did my best to rematch him with Davina,' Fiona Templeton said to Alexandra as they momentarily shared a mirror in the Ladies. 'But from what I gather, you had a real-life cupid on your side.'

Alexandra blinked at her, as much in surprise at the assumptions Fiona seemed to be making as at the puzzling reference.

'I mean the baby, my dear,' she said. 'We must meet for coffee one day,' she said pragmatically and sailed out to duty.

Was it that obvious? Alexandra wondered. Or had Riley said something to his mother? If so, what? As she returned to the table, Riley intercepted her, took her bag and stowed it and led her to the dance floor and, caught up in his arms, she found she didn't care.

There were other people on the floor but she and Riley turned slowly, insulated in a world of their own.

'That scent,' Riley said, breathing deep at her temple. 'What is it?'

She slid her cheek from his and looked up, exulted by the tension in his jaw. 'Does it make you think of things that are bound to be good for you? Like broccoli and prunes and oat bran? I'm such a wholesome gal, aren't I?'

'I am thinking of things that would be good for me,'

he admitted. His hands slid down to the upper slopes of her backside and pressed her close by way of illustration.

She gave a little gasp, her eyes widened. 'So you are.'

'And for you,' he replied softly.

Alexandra didn't remember a great deal about their departure. She retained an impression of gardens by moonlight and mild, night air on her skin and lights reflected on water. She remembered a piano playing over car speakers and a journey home through a familiar landscape that seemed suddenly as unfamiliar as another planet. Later, she couldn't recall arriving at her house, using a key, going inside.

But she would never forget the moment she turned into Riley's arms, knowing that this time she would never be the same when she left them again. Nor would she ever forget the sight of Riley shedding his jacket, tugging loose his bow tie by lamplight in her bedroom.

She gave a breathy little laugh, went and pushed his hands away. 'Let me. I've fantasised about undressing you—'

Riley's teeth flashed. He fell back on the bed, arms outstretched in mock submission. 'Here's your chance.'

Arrogant devil, she thought, surveying the length of him, the breadth of shoulder, the powerful features golden in the lamplight and etched with shadows. His hair had fallen forward over his forehead. Midnight blue eyes, half closed, glinted between thick, dark lashes. Stay me with flagons. Where to start?

No, she would never forget the pleasure of taking the initiative and kissing him, using the tip of her tongue to trace the outline of his lips before she tasted him. Riley made a rough sound in the back of his throat and kissed her back, but his arms remained spread wide.

And there was something unforgettable about looking into his eyes as she unknotted his tie, pulled its silky length through her fingers to toss it on the floor. She knelt by him in her silky dress, to unfasten his shirt.

Riley hitched himself on his elbows to take the shirt off, but she had embarked on an exploration of the lovely contours of his chest and there he stayed, the fine, tucked shirt exposing his big shoulders and the strong lines of his flung-back neck and head.

And her memory would hoard the sound of Riley saying her name and every move of his expressive hands as they played over her body, peeling the thin, silken layers of her clothes from her. And her own voice, husky and deep, saying, 'Let me,' when he unbuckled his belt and unzipped his pants.

Riley lay back and watched her through half-closed eyes, wanting more of the subtle pleasures of Alexandra's hands and mouth as she removed his trousers. He loved the way she watched the result of her every move with such intensity, the way she traced the newly exposed skin of his stomach and thighs with her fingertips. It was like the drift of a smoking feather over his skin, leaving a trail of fire.

She chucked the trousers on the floor, looked deep in his eyes then turned her attention to his briefs. Very slowly, very deliberately, she laid both hands on him.

'Alexandra—' He supposed he must have said her name. She cradled him through the thin fabric and he felt himself throb against her hands, dragged himself back from the precipice, cold with fear that he might not make it.

He sat up, braced against the headboard and pulled her up with him, parting her beautiful, pale thighs so that she was face to face with him, wrapped around him but not yet completely. He sweated. It was possibly the most important night of his life. He wanted it to be so right, so good, that his confidence almost deserted him.

But Alexandra whispered, 'Riley,' and he filled his hands with the wondrous, wide-stretched curves of her backside and held her still for a moment. Then he lowered her, inch by inch, and the look in her eyes and her ragged rushes of breath restored him. He smiled at her, caught back the cloud of bronzed hair from her damp forehead and said softly, 'No hurry, my love. We've got all night.'

No, she'd not forget the night. Or the way Riley brought her to the brink time and again, laughing at her pleas, delighting in his mastery until she took matters into her own hands. And this time was no slow tease but a magnificent plunging, runaway affair that dragged the breath from her body in incoherent cries on the ride of her life.

Correction. Rides.

That Sunday they went out walking, arms around each other, for hours, then ate and made love with the sunlight shafting across the bed in a broad stripe, and there seemed no end to their pleasure in each other.

Riley spent every night in her bed, until Sam returned home. Then he moved into his finished apartment to tidy it up so that Alexandra could spend her nights with him.

Before he went, he asked her to marry him.

She wanted to say yes, but she hesitated.

Riley's eyes narrowed.

'Um—well—we haven't known each other very long,' she offered.

His expression was sceptical as well it might be. Their relationship had matured fast, accelerated by the unusual presence of a baby in their earliest dealings with each other. You learned a great deal about someone by watching them with a child, or someone with no power, more than you might learn in months, even years, otherwise. No, the length of their relationship was not the problem.

Alexandra had hesitated because she hadn't quite cut the habit of clinging to that fading picture.

'No matter,' said Riley briskly, watching her. 'Let me know whenever you make up your mind.'

* * *

Sam returned with a hundredweight of reunion photographs. The goats came back in the truck and Sam pronounced his herd and especially Millie, his best milker, fit as fiddles. Alexandra stayed nights with Riley in his lushly renovated apartment, but his unanswered question hung between them, taking the edge off their happiness.

'I'll be playing at the club tomorrow night,' he said, a week after Sam had returned. 'Why don't I call in at the shop after closing, the night after that?'

It was the first time she'd been alone since the night of the CUFF dinner. She found she didn't like it.

The next evening, the arcade shops had mostly closed when Alexandra went out to pack up her customer 'bait' books from the table outside the window. Some strange energy in the air alerted her to Riley's presence. She looked up and saw him coming her way. Her spirits lifted at the sight of him but she felt the usual struggle between the two competing images that plagued her. Riley, in vibrant flesh and blood, and the fading picture of the future that she'd been so certain was hers.

She waved to him and watched as someone tried to catch up with him. Alexandra transferred two books from the table to her trolley, uncertain at which point she became uneasy. Perhaps when a second man appeared, running to catch up with Riley. He carried something and there was something warlike about the way he did it.

'Riley—' she yelled, pointing behind him. *A baseball bat.* The second man had a baseball bat, was raising it. *'Riley!'* she screeched.

But as Riley turned his head the two men reached him and the bat swiped in a vicious arc. Riley staggered, lashed out at one of the men, who head-butted him and pushed him to the ground in front of the batsman. The bat swung up.

It was a moment of clarity. There was no mental

struggle, no competing vision in her mind. There was only Riley. And the chance that she could lose him.

'No—o—o,' she howled as she ran, dropping books from her arms until only one remained clutched in her hand. Distracted by the banshee cry, the aggressor hesitated and she barrelled up to him and clouted him with the sturdy hardcover she held. He reeled and staggered away in the wake of his bolting, unarmed accomplice.

Alexandra fell to her knees beside Riley.

'You're *bleeding!*' she whispered. 'Oh, God, Riley—please be all right. I love you and I want to live with you, spend my life with you.'

A small crowd had gathered. A police officer showed up and took descriptions of the attackers. Riley, a plaster from Alexandra's first-aid kit applied over his cheekbone, made several phone calls from the bookshop phone.

It was, he told Alexandra, more than likely that the two men were the ones responsible for vandalising his apartment.

'I took a prosecution case against their cousin late last year. He got a five-year prison sentence and was beaten up by inmates a few weeks back. They'd already wrecked my apartment so this time they targeted me. Blamed me I suppose for the boy being in jail. Bloody fools,' Riley said in angry resignation. 'They've only brought more trouble on their family.'

Wincing, he pulled her into his arms. 'I seem to remember you babbling something about wanting to spend the rest of your life with me when I lay wounded on the ground. Does that mean you will marry me?'

Alexandra kissed him. 'Yes.'

She must have imagined the flash of uncertainty in his eyes because a moment later he grinned and said, 'And now, I think it only fair that I buy the book that made such an impact on my baseball-bat-wielding friend.'

Alexandra had great satisfaction in delivering into his hands the copy of Rev. W. Morley Punshon's *Sermons*.

'My God, you booksellers will do anything to shift unsold stock,' said Riley.

CHAPTER TEN

IT WAS a fine May night and the riverside paths of Southbank were peopled with joggers and parents trailing lively toddlers, with those ambling on foot, or in wheelchair, with tourists sharing guidebooks, with lovers sharing looks. A man bore a sign that said the world was about to end, another that Huang's fish and chips were on special.

The *Kookaburra Queen* honked its riverboat horn and passed by, fragmenting the reflections of Brisbane city lights on the opposite bank.

On a forecourt under a canopy, the portraits competing for a new art prize were hung on zigzagged screens and the public, plied with the sponsor's free samples of its up-market soft drinks, imagined themselves art lovers and critics.

Alexandra walked across the Victoria Bridge from the city to Southbank. The breeze was soft on her face and she would have paused in the centre to take in the view except that Riley would already be there, and her mother's portrait of him that she still had not seen.

She looked first for the man but didn't find him. But she found her mother's likeness of him. She rounded a screen and came face to face with the portrait. The emotional punch of it took her breath away.

It was a large canvas and the image near life-size. This was no formal picture of Riley Templeton, Barrister. His mother would be disappointed that he was not wearing court robes and a wig. Riley wore no jacket, his shirt sleeves were rolled up, his top buttons unfastened. Around his neck, his unknotted tie hung down as he knelt on the floor and an infant's fingers were raised, ready to close on the strip of silk fabric.

Riley and Savannah, in wordless communication. The grown adult, temporarily divested of suspicion and cynicism, the infant as yet unfamiliar with distrust. Rhona had painted a faint curve to Riley's mouth but the smile was in the eyes and tenderness was in every line of strong shoulders and arms that curved to and around the tiny child. It had no title, but it could have been called 'Fatherhood.'

Alexandra scrubbed tears from her eyes as she sensed someone approaching. She turned and there was Riley with the smile in his eyes and the lines of shoulder and arms curving toward her. That was more than any woman could want, but Rhona had shown her a future that she had already grieved for and now she grieved again for herself, and for Riley. And for Riley's child. What a father he would have been.

He tried to slow himself down as he approached her. If he had done what came naturally he would have run that last ten metres, as eager as a kid to get to her. He felt a physical pain, right in the gut. Was this how it was going to be? Would he always be conscious of the fact that he loved her more than she loved him? If she loved him at all.

Riley rejected that last. Of course she loved him. But then, Alexandra loved so readily. Stray kids, her elderly neighbour, pensioned customers, new hobbies. Was he just another stray that she loved along with the rest? Another hobby to be relegated to the fireplace with the other remnants of past passions? Or had she, after all, talked herself into loving him because he fitted some crazy notion of a suitable 'life partner'? Maybe a deadly combination of the two.

His usually ordered mind grappled with it. She had said she'd marry him at a time of heightened emotion,

when she had seen him hurt and felt sorry for him, and
that bothered him. But he would be bothered, too, if she
had accepted him in cool, rational detachment as a good
prospect. So what the hell did he want?

He gave himself the supreme pleasure of holding her
for a moment, murmured a greeting into her ear and
breathed the fragrance of her hair. Alexandra glanced up
at him. There were tears in her eyes.

'My mother doesn't miss a thing,' she said, sniffing.
'She's shown you in the middle of undressing, as usual.'
She kissed him quickly on the mouth and turned to look
again at the portrait.

She looked emotional, evasive. He felt the kick in his
solar plexus. For the first time he became aware that he
was expecting her to reject him. Not at this moment
perhaps. But some moment, some day.

'That pose was a killer for the back muscles and the
neck,' Riley said casually. He studied the canvas, aware
that Alexandra was taking quick looks at him, as if she
was trying to bring herself to say something. To tell him
she'd made a mistake? But she would be kind, would
let him down lightly. Riley closed his eyes for a moment,
anticipating the pain of it, feeling it in his gut. 'Riley,'
she would say, 'it won't work. But can we remain good
friends?' Out of the corner of his eye, he saw her open
her mouth. Here it comes.

'It's not fair!' she burst out. The tissue disintegrated
and she thrust it into her bag and fished for another.
Riley found a handkerchief and put it in her hand.

'Does Rhona's work always affect you like this?' he
asked. 'And what's not fair?'

'People who couldn't care less can have children!
People who don't even bother to look after them!'

'Yes, my thoughts exactly.' Relief. This wasn't to be
the moment. Something had moved her, some evidence
of neglect, or some outrage to her sense of justice. He
relaxed.

Alexandra whirled, taking him by surprise. She grasped his arms and gazed intensely into his eyes. His stomach lurched sickeningly. God. Wrong again.

'Riley—' She hesitated and he could see her mentally considering and rejecting words. Was that what she had been doing when he came upon her? Rehearsing words of goodbye with tears in her eyes? Riley was seized by a comradely compassion for all those people he had seen, standing in court, waiting to hear the verdict that would determine their life.

And somehow he was going to have to stay calm. Somehow he was going to have to resist knocking over those screens, pulling out those clumps of lilies by the roots, snatching that sign about the end of the world and smashing it into fragments.

'This is difficult—we've never talked about it, *I've* never brought it up before because I know you don't like to talk about it—but—'

She chewed on her lip. There was pain and, yes, pity in her eyes. His desolate anger escalated. Just one clump of lilies, then. Just one swipe at them before he went. He'd always hated lilies.

'I mean—I've always wanted them and I've got used to the idea now of not having them—at least not the usual way—um—'

In his mind's eye, Riley saw the long green leaves of the lilies in shreds. After that, he would get drunk at the club. And play piano till dawn or oblivion, whichever came first.

'And I know you have strong feelings about it and you might never want to—um—'

Riley frowned at her and she rushed on, as if trying to appease him.

'But I thought when you've had time to think about it, you might consider—um—'

'What, Alexandra?' he snapped. 'For God's sake, get

on with it but don't expect me to pave the way. Consider what?'

She licked her lips, squared her shoulders and her fingers shifted and tightened on his arms. Riley didn't think he could bear much more of her compassion and regret.

'Adoption,' she said at last.

Her eyes were anxiously on him, assessing his reaction. Her hands had begun a soothing kind of motion on his arms. Alexandra was nervously silent. Riley stared at her, trying to make the word match any one of the several he'd expected to hear.

Over. Mistake. Sorry. Goodbye.

He was silent, unable to make any sense of it.

Alexandra burst into speech. 'Look, I shouldn't have brought this up, it isn't the time or the place. And I don't want you to think that I haven't got used to the idea of never having any because I have. It wasn't easy but I *am* used to it now, Riley.'

His mind, used to processing complex sets of facts at top speed, ground along like one of Sam's rusting farm implements.

'Adoption?' he said, plucking out what seemed the operative word here.

'There are other ways, too, but a lot of men couldn't stand the idea of sperm banks and I'm not sure I could myself. And adoption's not the same as having your own natural child, but fatherhood isn't just being able to conceive a child—it's being a father every day, caring and helping and teaching and loving and—all the things you do so well.'

'Sperm banks?' Riley said faintly.

She looked at the portrait, then at him. 'When I saw that, I just thought—but I know you might never like the idea, adoption I mean, and if you don't, I just want you to know that I won't be so obsessed about being childless that I'll end up like Anna Brown, trying to steal someone else's baby.'

One phrase leapt out at Riley. *Fatherhood isn't just being able to conceive a child.* A certain analytical ability returned to him. He examined the phrase, set it against other telling words and phrases in Alexandra's garbled outburst. *People who couldn't care less can have children. Childless. It wasn't easy but I've got used to it. Adoption. You might never like the idea.* Cautiously, he cast his mind back several months over conversations, Alexandra's plans for a large family, her immense compassion towards him on certain occasions. Come to think of it, when was the last time she had mentioned that large family to him?

He reached an inescapable conclusion, but was suspicious of it because it was too good to be true. He opened and closed his mouth several times.

'Riley,' she said, sliding her arms around his waist. 'I love you. Why don't we just play it by ear?'

'You've always wanted kids,' he said. There was a lump in his throat. She couldn't mean what he thought she meant, surely? Riley tested for weaknesses. 'You're the earthmother type, you *should* have children. It would be a tragedy if you didn't.'

'It would be a tragedy if I didn't marry you,' she said into his neck.

'You—still want to marry me, live your life with me, even if I—can't give you children?'

Alexandra looked up at him, puzzled. 'Of course. But you already know that.'

And still he tested, pushing to the limit, hating himself for his greed. 'Even if—I can't bring myself to adopt a child?'

She kissed him on the mouth, and said, 'Yes. Even then.' Then she looked beyond him and with a final squeeze of his hand, she hurried over to Rhona who had just been released from a group of well-wishers and critics. In the distance he saw Pam and Jeff approaching with Savannah in her pushchair.

Riley stood there in front of the painting of himself for a long time, attracting attention from passers-by who noticed the resemblance. Even now, he might have it all wrong. Was he trying to interpret Alexandra's ramblings to suit himself? After a while, Rhona came and stood beside him.

'I don't think I'll win,' she told him. 'Pity, I could use the prize money. Although I know I can do without a year's supply of Fruifiz, the soft drink for grown-ups.'

At a distance, Pam and Jeff flanked Alexandra, who had Savannah installed on her hip and was pointing out a boat on the river. Alexandra's curly head was bent towards the little girl and even from here, her tenderness was incandescent.

'Do you look forward to having grandchildren, Rhona?' he asked.

She gave him a shrewd look. 'Is that your way of asking if I'm disappointed that you're sterile?' she asked in her straightforward way.

'Did Alexandra tell you that?'

She nodded. 'Eventually.'

A party of three advanced on them with outstretched hands and Rhona's name on their lips. Riley moved away before he could be caught up in conversation. Into comparative darkness he walked, down the slope towards the river. Alone, he stared at the myriad city lights, then the stars that outnumbered them.

Alexandra, warm and generous, loved him enough to abandon her dreams. Sweat broke out on his forehead, although a breeze came, cooled by the river. He disliked himself for having doubted her, for needing a sign that she loved him, and he was humbled that he had been given such a sign.

For a long time Riley stayed by the river, contemplating humility and the nature of love, the beauty of lilies and the sad mistakenness of the man whose sign predicted the end of the world.

* * *

He stood with his hands in his pockets, still as a statue, his broad shoulders and the distinctive shape of his head outlined against the river's shattered silver. Alexandra had watched his stillness uneasily for some time but now she walked down to him. Had she stirred up bitterness in him by bringing up the subject of his inability to have children?

'Riley,' she said softly.

He turned and took her hand. His eyes glittered with so much reflected light that it looked for a moment like tears. He smiled and the flash of his teeth was robust, confident.

'The name of the song is "Veracity,"' he told her. 'The song that goes around in your head in the small hours of the morning. The one you feel sure you know but whose words you can't recall.'

She frowned. '"Veracity." No, the title doesn't ring any bells. And yet I'm sure I know it. It's so familiar—'

'And it doesn't have any words.'

'Oh. I could have sworn it did. Are you sure?'

'Very sure. I wrote the music. I didn't write any words.'

'*You* wrote it?'

He pulled her in close, put his mouth to her hair. 'And it couldn't possibly be familiar to you, my darling girl. You only heard it once. The fact that you were singing my song and certain you knew the words to it when you couldn't possibly...I felt that was a sign.'

'A sign? I didn't think you legal types were so intuitive.'

'"Hopeful" would be more accurate. I was hopeful that it meant something, especially as you were so unimpressed with my virtuoso performance.'

She raised demure eyes to his. 'Which virtuoso performance was that?'

He grinned, slid his hands down to her hips and tipped her hard against him by way of reminder.

'Ah,' she said reminiscently. '*That* virtuoso performance…was I impressed? You might have to refresh my memory as to the details…'

Riley took her hand and walked to the nearest tree, edged her against the trunk in the canopy's shadow and refreshed her memory. He demonstrated his one-handed expertise with small buttons. Also the expertise of performing two quite separate actions with each hand, the mark of a practicing pianist. In no time at all, Alexandra felt the breeze, cool on her bare skin, then Riley's mouth, warm and questing, caressing, taking small, sensitive bits of her inside to taste and suck and drive her to stifled sighs of pleasure.

Voices approached, and Riley demonstrated his equal expertise at buttoning up small buttons and simultaneously smoothing mussed hair. By the time a family passed by to the river, led by two children, Riley and Alexandra were fit for public viewing and if their breathing was a little heavy, the sounds of late-night-shopping traffic on the bridge masked it.

Passion postponed, they watched the bobbing figures of the children, tended by their parents.

'I hope,' Alexandra said tentatively, 'I didn't upset you too much tonight, when I—'

Riley put a finger to her lips. 'Alexandra, there's been a—misunderstanding.'

She looked anxious. 'I *have* upset you. Look, I won't bring the subject up again unless you do, okay?'

Riley shook his head, gave a peculiar sort of guffaw. What was wrong with him?

'Alexandra—I am not sterile.'

She blinked several times. 'What?'

'There is nothing wrong with my—erm—that is, I have every reason to believe that my, ah, apparatus is in perfect working order.'

'What?' Alexandra stared blankly at him.

'I don't know how else to put it. I can procreate. I am fertile. I can be a father.'

She continued to stare at him in silence, drew back out of his arms so that only his hands rested lightly on her waist.

'But you said—when we first met—that you'd never had a baby and you never would.'

'I didn't say I never *could*.'

'You *said*,' she went on, moving again so that his hands fell to his sides. 'You *told* me you couldn't have children!'

'You assumed it.' Riley's voice had taken on a firmer note.

She turned away towards the river and the city, a hand to her forehead, whirled back to face him. 'I apologised to you for reminding you that you couldn't have kids, and you said—'

'I said, ''There is no need to feel sympathy for me'' or something along those lines,' Riley said. 'Surely that was plain enough—that your sympathy was out of place because I didn't have the problem.'

'You were *upset* every time the subject of kids came up. You were morose when you spoke about your ex-wife with her children. You were sad because you were thinking they could have been yours—*if circumstances were different!*'

He snorted. 'Yes, they could have been mine if I'd been daft enough to rush into having kids at twenty-two—and then I would have been responsible for putting that pinched look on their faces when I divorced their mother! If I was sad, it was because I could so easily have brought a couple of kids into the world only to make them miserable.'

Alexandra's temper rose as he countered her every interpretation with his flat, rational explanations. 'You said *more people should be sterile* because too many kids were badly treated—I was justified in thinking you included yourself in their number!' she accused.

'A figure of speech,' he said calmly. 'You jumped to your conclusion early on—a spectacular leap I might say—and everything you heard after that simply supported it. It's always a dangerous mistake to—'

Alexandra lashed out at him, caught him on the shoulder with the flat of her hand. Riley staggered.

'*Don't* you dare lecture me, you pompous—!' She stared at him, breathing hard, her cheeks hot. 'You let me think that you couldn't—let me believe that we'd never—and I've spent the worst months of my life trying to come to terms with something that just isn't *true!* I've gone through *agony,* and you just stand there and tell me it's all my own fault because I got it wrong!' So furious was she that she lashed out again but this time Riley caught her wrist.

'Alexandra,' he said, biting out the name. 'I am leaving now to go to the club. We'll talk about this when you've had time to calm down.'

'Don't be so damned patronising,' she hissed.

'When we've both calmed down,' he amended, though his expression was not in the least apologetic. Riley, in fact, looked supremely arrogant. He walked away, lengthening his stride to outdistance her as she hurried alongside, directing furious accusations of falsehood at him until to continue would have been to create a scene among her mother's friends.

Riley said a few words to Rhona, to Jeff and Pam, briefly shook one of Savannah's chubby fists, then strode off. Alexandra stared after him, then, catching her mother's speculative eye, walked off ostensibly to view the other exhibits. A brisk circuit of the artworks brought Rhona to her side.

'Trouble in paradise?' her mother asked.

'He's *not* sterile!' Alexandra burst out. 'Can you believe it?'

Rhona blinked. 'Oh.'

'I mean, right from the start he let me think…and he was always so damned sensitive about the subject so I didn't dwell on it…and it was obvious from everything he said that he couldn't have kids!' she fumed. 'And now he, he looks down that oversized nose of his and tells me that I—' She stabbed herself several times on the chest with an index finger. '*I* was mistaken. Mistaken!'

Her mother shook her head. 'Tch. Patronising.'

'I've been in torment—he has no idea! I've dreamed about his children, our family and bit by bit, day by day, I've come to terms with not having them… It was like having a fabulous picture and painting over it piece by piece until it was gone. And he doesn't even seem to think I have any right to be angry!'

'Oh, that's inexcusable. You've made such an effort and now you find the blackguard is fertile? Perhaps he could have the op, so it won't all have been in vain.' She mimed a scissor motion—the unkindest cut of all.

Alexandra stared blankly at her. 'He's not sterile after all,' she repeated as by rote.

'Hmmm, well you shouldn't get your hopes up, if you pardon the pun. Sperm count levels have gone down all around the world, I believe—'

'He's *not* sterile,' Alexandra said again. She laughed. 'He can have children.' Alexandra took her mother's hands, swung in a small circle. 'He can have children!'

'And I'm very happy for you both,' Rhona said. 'In fact the whole of the Southbank is happy to hear it.' She hugged Alexandra, then stepped aside. 'Go after him. Don't wait for the awards ceremony—I won't win and there are all those speeches and several hundred litres of Fruifiz to get through—'

A few early jazz lovers clustered about the piano. It was early yet and the smoke haze was immature, so

Alexandra could make out Riley's head, bent low over
the keyboard. His jacket was draped over the open dou-
ble-bass case, his vest was entirely unbuttoned, his shirt
partially. His silk tie was stuffed into a trouser pocket,
the protruding tail trembling to the beat of one large foot.

She stood by the piano and smiled down at this big,
untidy man who so often looked as if he was getting
ready for bed.

'Riley,' she said. The fan next to her frowned and
said, 'Sssh.' Alexandra tapped her fingers on the piano
top and she was the only person in the cellar not in time
with the music. The fan showed the whites of his eyes.

The number came to its roundabout close and Riley
unfolded, flexed his shoulders. No cigarette this time. He
raised his eyes to hers.

'*Deja vu.*'

'I have to talk to you,' she said. 'About a baby.'

'You've got one—or you want one?'

'I want one.'

The fan, waiting for the next number, looked bored
with the conversation.

'Oh, yeah?' said Riley, with a glance at him. 'Just like
that? You want to have a kid with musical talent so you
come in here propositioning me to combine my genes
with yours?'

'For a fee,' Alexandra protested, playing to the gleam
in Riley's eyes. 'I've looked around and you're the best
prospect I've seen.'

'Is that right?'

'You're in good physical shape, not bad-looking, decent voice, no obvious flaws and you've got—erm—'

'Big antlers?'

'Absolutely.'

The fan raised a brow but took this in his stride.
Alexandra looked for any of the signs of uneasiness that
Riley had shown in the past about this kind of mercenary
assessment. There was not a trace. Of course there

wouldn't be, would there? Riley Templeton knew she could never have made a commonsense, mercenary decision about him. He knew exactly how much she loved him. Exactly how much she had been prepared to give up for him. Riley's confidence was at an all-time high.

'Of course, pomposity and a tendency to arrogance runs in your family, but they're probably not genetic,' she said with a sniff as the smoke in the air got to her.

The fan folded his arms and tapped one foot.

'I did have some reservations about the nose,' she went on, indicating his excessively noble feature. 'But I'm prepared to take a chance on that.'

'Big of you.'

The fan looked at his watch and sighed.

'So—when do you want to do the deed?' Riley enquired.

Alexandra looked around and spread her hands in a gesture that said no time like the present. 'Is there somewhere private here?'

'Sure. I can clear the desk in the office.' Riley stood up and reached for his jacket.

The fan came to attention. 'You're not going *now?*' he complained. 'In the middle of a bracket? Can't you *wait?*' he demanded of Alexandra.

'Some things are more important than jazz,' she said, straight-faced.

And the unshockable fan was shocked at last.

Riley exchanged words with the bass player and slipped away with Alexandra. Fortitude Valley hummed with traffic as the Friday night club scene warmed up and the late-night shoppers moved on to cafes and bars and Chinatown restaurants.

They walked and now Riley was serious at last.

'I wasn't sure if you loved me,' he admitted. 'You're the kind of woman who *wants* to love, the kind who gets involved with people, especially lame ducks, and I thought you might be sorry for me—'

She laughed. 'Riley, no one in their right mind would think of you as a lame duck.'

'You always gave me that look, so compassionate, full of pity or regret or something and I thought, "Anytime now she's going to tell me it's all over, that she felt sorry for me and mistook it for love." On the other hand, I thought maybe you had weighed up my virtues against Graham's and I had proved a better prospect as a life partner. But I didn't know, you see, that you thought I couldn't give you children. Didn't know *that* was why you looked at me with that dying swan expression—'

Alexandra made a snorting noise in the back of her throat.

'Dying swan!' she muttered.

'Tonight, when I realised that you thought that marrying me could mean never having kids...I was— I felt—' He looked away, up at the stars, as if seeking elusive words. It seemed a long time before he said, 'Humble.'

But his humility had fast turned to triumph, Alexandra thought, remembering his almost overbearing assurance on the riverbank, his near-swagger as he left, confident that she would follow. Life with Riley was going to be nothing if not a challenge.

But for now, Riley was reliving a rare moment of humility and the look in his eyes took her breath away.

'To be loved by you, Alexandra Page—' he said softly. His fingertips brushed curling strands of hair from her forehead. 'I'm a lucky man.'

'Hmmm. For a while there I was certain you were going to marry Davina—again.' Alexandra frowned as she remembered her mother giving that distinct impression. Had Rhona been giving her a little push in Riley's direction? Poor Fiona Templeton. She had been working

on a rematch between her son and Davina unaware of
the powerful forces ranged against her.

'And I actually believed you might marry the gormless Graham.'

'He's not gormless,' she protested.

'He doesn't make a move without setting his stop-
watch. Making love with him must have been a math-
ematical business. Does he time it? Take his pulse first,
then afterwards?'

She snuggled up to him, smiling. Riley's confidence
wasn't one hundred percent, after all. 'I wouldn't know,'
she said.

His eyes glittered. 'You mean—?'

'He was in training—wasn't he?—for the triathlon.'

'You mean when he's in training, he doesn't—'

'No coffee, no alcohol, no sex.'

'None at all? Must have been hard,' said Riley.

'I wouldn't know,' Alexandra said again, demurely.

He chuckled. 'You let me think you and he were
sleeping together.'

'You *assumed*, Riley,' she said, taking a pedantic
tone. 'You jumped to conclusions early on and everything you heard after that supported your belief. It's always a dangerous mistake.'

They reached the car park. 'Are we going somewhere?' she asked.

'To my place. If I'm going to combine my genes with
yours, I need to rehearse.'

'You are the one who can think on your feet and
doesn't need to rehearse.'

'But then, I wasn't intending to be on my feet...'
Riley was thoughtful, reviewing the possibilities. 'However, there is no evidence to suggest that it can't be done
and, in fact, I believe there may even be precedents—'

The smell of crushed thyme wafted on the spring air as
dozens of ankles stirred the borders of Alexandra's herb

garden. Further to the front, Sam's plum trees were thick
with blossom and ecstatic bees. There were some bleat-
ings from beyond the paddock and an occasional com-
mentary from Sam's best milker who stood looking over
the fence at the party and foraging in the tall grass and
blown debris lodged around the wire mesh.

'Now what's my Millie eating?' said Sam, going to
investigate as the nanny munched on something unrec-
ognizable.

In the centre, near the sundial, stood a stout table piled
with food and a limitless supply of Fruifiz. Raised above
the chicken wings and salads and morsels of cheese and
smoked salmon, was a birthday cake covered in green
icing and decorated with a foil pond inscribed with
'Happy Birthday Savannah.' Several small, green, fon-
dant frogs crouched in a clump of pink icing waterlilies.
There was one pink candle.

Cameras clicked as Savannah tottered a few steps in
her new, white shoes, delighted with her own cleverness
and all the attention. She sat down heavily on a patch
of sage.

'Savannah…look this way for Uncle Riley,' Riley
called, and Alexandra looked down at him where he
crouched with the camera. He took the photograph and
the little girl lurched towards him, her feet hardly ap-
pearing to touch the ground in that odd way that the
newest walkers had, as if they were not yet quite
grounded. He handed the camera to Alexandra, opened
his arms and the little girl ran into them, squealing as
he rose and lifted her high in the air.

Alexandra looked at them through the viewfinder,
Riley and Savannah laughing at each other, the man and
the baby in perfect harmony.

'You're going to make a wonderful father,' she told
him when Pam reclaimed her daughter and moved towards the birthday cake.

Riley took the camera back and raised it for a picture of Pam and Savannah with the untouched birthday cake.

'Maybe, in time. I'm just practising.'

'Will—em—nine months be long enough?' she enquired.

'Pam.' Riley waved Pam over to his left and set his eye to the window. 'Ah—that's great. Hold that pose.'

Pam held the pose. Riley held his. His eye remained at the viewfinder, his index finger remained poised over the button. At last he turned his head. 'What did you say?'

'Hurry, Riley,' warned Pam as Savannah wriggled to extend one chubby arm towards the cake. Pam restrained the questing hand but the move was a feint. With her other hand Savannah reached down and swiped a channel through the gleaming green cream. A frog plopped onto the tablecloth. Savannah conveyed a green splodge to her mouth and happily sucked her fingers. Riley didn't take the photo but the video camera whirred.

Sam returned to the group, holding the food source wrested from his best milker.

'See,' he said, giving it to Alexandra. 'I *told* you I left a note. Must have blown away.'

She glanced at it to please Sam. It was the back of a cornflakes carton that had been damped by rain and dried by sun many times since it had caught in the fence. Snails had left their trails over the surfaces but there were faint traces of Sam's writing left. She could make out her own name and 'stay' and 'keys' and 'Riley.'

Riley looked at Sam's note, too, but when the old man had moved away, he turned his attention to Alexandra. 'What did you say?'

She looked into his eyes. Riley's baby would probably have his eyes of darkest blue. Alexandra smiled at him, laid her hands on his lovely shoulders.

'I'm not one hundred percent certain...' she admitted, checking for his reaction. Riley had had such a lot to say about the perils of parenthood, about not wanting to risk it. 'I've missed before and it's been nothing…'

Riley studied her long and seriously. He removed her hands from his neck and held them. Sam's snail-bitten note crumbled.

'Riley?' she said as her spirits sank. 'Are you upset? I shouldn't have said anything yet…it might not be a baby…'

He swallowed, raised her hands to his lips and kissed them.

'I hope it is,' he said at last. 'We've already mastered the art of Bathing Baby and Washing Baby's Hair. It would be a pity to waste all that expertise.'

She laughed, drew him a little away from the others. 'Do you think we'll be okay, Riley, you and I? You always said too many people were rotten parents. Will you have regrets?'

'I don't know,' he said honestly, and drew her into his arms to smile down at her. 'But I know we're in this for the long haul. We have to be.' He took the tattered piece of cereal packet from her, tossed it over the fence to where Sam's best milker waited. 'Our names are on the note.'

HARLEQUIN PRESENTS®

HARLEQUIN PRESENTS
men you won't be able to resist
falling in love with...

HARLEQUIN PRESENTS
women who have feelings
just like your own...

HARLEQUIN PRESENTS
powerful passion in
exotic international settings...

HARLEQUIN PRESENTS
intense, dramatic stories that will keep you
turning to the very last page...

HARLEQUIN PRESENTS
The world's bestselling romance series!

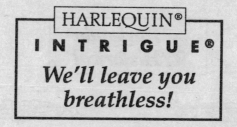

LOOK FOR OUR FOUR FABULOUS MEN!

Each month some of today's bestselling authors bring
four new fabulous men to Harlequin American Romance.
Whether they're rebel ranchers, millionaire power brokers
or sexy single dads, they're all gallant princes—and
they're all ready to sweep you into lighthearted fantasies
and contemporary fairy tales where anything is possible
and where all your dreams come true!

You don't even have to make a wish…
Harlequin American Romance will grant your every desire!

Look for Harlequin American Romance
wherever Harlequin books are sold!

Harlequin Romance®

Delightful

Affectionate

Romantic

Emotional

Tender

Original

Daring

Riveting

Enchanting

Adventurous

Moving

Harlequin Romance—the
series that has it all!

HROM-G